DEATH OF A
TURKEY

KATE BORDEN

BERKLEY PRIME CRIME, NEW YORK

THE BERKLEY PUBLISHING GROUP
Published by the Penguin Group
Penguin Group (USA) Inc.
375 Hudson Street, New York, New York 10014, USA
Penguin Group (Canada), 90 Eglinton Avenue East, Suite 700, Toronto, Ontario M4P 2Y3, Canada
(a division of Pearson Penguin Canada Inc.)
Penguin Books Ltd., 80 Strand, London WC2R 0RL, England
Penguin Group Ireland, 25 St. Stephen's Green, Dublin 2, Ireland (a division of Penguin Books Ltd.)
Penguin Group (Australia), 250 Camberwell Road, Camberwell, Victoria 3124, Australia
(a division of Pearson Australia Group Pty. Ltd.)
Penguin Books India Pvt. Ltd., 11 Community Centre, Panchsheel Park, New Delhi—110 017, India
Penguin Group (NZ), Cnr. Airborne and Rosedale Roads, Albany, Auckland 1310, New Zealand
(a division of Pearson New Zealand Ltd.)
Penguin Books (South Africa) (Pty.) Ltd., 24 Sturdee Avenue, Rosebank, Johannesburg 2196, South Africa

Penguin Books Ltd., Registered Offices: 80 Strand, London WC2R 0RL, England

DEATH OF A TURKEY

A Berkley Prime Crime Book / published by arrangement with the author

PRINTING HISTORY
Berkley Prime Crime mass-market edition / August 2005

Copyright © 2005 by The Berkley Publishing Group.
Cover design by Erica Tricarico.
Cover art by Dan Craig.
Interior text design by Kristin del Rosario.

ISBN: 0-425-20446-4

BERKLEY® PRIME CRIME
Berkley Prime Crime Books are published by The Berkley Publishing Group,
a division of Penguin Group (USA) Inc.,
375 Hudson Street, New York, New York 10014.
The name BERKLEY PRIME CRIME and the BERKLEY PRIME CRIME design are trademarks belonging to Penguin Group (USA) Inc.

PRINTED IN THE UNITED STATES OF AMERICA

10 9 8 7 6 5 4 3 2 1

For Pam, Tom, Will, Sally and Alice;
Bill and Marilyn with love and thanks
for the best Thanksgiving gravy recipe
ever invented.

CHAPTER 1

ON A FROSTY NOVEMBER MORNING, PEGGY JEAN
Turner awoke filled with a delicious sense of antici-
pation. Her favorite holiday was less than two weeks
away, and she had the day planned down to the last
crumb of pumpkin pie. It was time to make her
Thanksgiving shopping list.

She slipped out of the cozy cocoon of her flannel-
covered comforter and went to the window. Pulling
back the curtains, Peggy grinned when she saw frost
flakes etched on the pane. Pressing her nose against
the cold glass, she squealed with delight at the sight
of her yard filled with fresh, untrampled snow.

Winter had come to Cobb's Landing.

Pausing just long enough to jam her feet into slippers, Peggy flew down the stairs—being careful not
to wake her eleven-year-old son Nicky, who liked to
sleep late on Saturday mornings—and opened her

back door. She sniffed the crisp air, laced with spicy pine from the trees bordering her yard. Twenty-eight degrees and no wind. A perfect New England winter morning.

Peggy pranced on tip-toe through the snow to the middle of her yard. She dropped on her back, closed her eyes, and slowly moved her arms and legs, smiling as she made a snow angel. *Ahhh.* She exhaled a sigh of pure contentment.

Whoosh! A loosely packed snowball flew over Peggy's head, landing with a soft plop near the angel's left wing. Peggy grinned and called out to her best friend and next-door neighbor, Lavinia Cooper. "Coffee, Lovey, I need coffee."

Lavinia laughed. "Come and get it. But don't track snow in my clean kitchen." Lavinia shivered, hugging herself to keep warm. "It's cold out here. I'm going back inside."

Trying to keep her perfect snow angel intact, Peggy rose to her elbows but was shoved back into the snow by what felt like a cannonball landing on her chest. Gasping for breath, Peggy looked down at an enormous black and white short-haired cat. The cat hissed, glaring at Peggy through slitted amber eyes.

From a distance came an unfamiliar voice. "Holstein, you naughty kitty. Holstein, where are you? Come back this instant."

The cat flipped its long bushy tail, then trotted through the snow, pausing to squat and relieve itself before bounding over the fence, looking to Peggy like a cow jumping over the moon. Hey, diddle diddle.

Nicky appeared barefoot at the back door in his flannel pajamas, rubbing sleep from his eyes. "Mom, there's someone banging on the front door."

"Who is it, Nicky?"

"I dunno. Some lady." Nicky yawned and went back into the house.

Brushing snow from the sweat suit she slept in— an economy measure to keep her winter heating bills below the national debt—Peggy went through her house to the front door. There stood a squat woman in a puffy brown coat, a badly knit orange cap perched on her head. Cradled in her arms was the black and white cat.

"Hope I didn't get you up. I'm Prunella Post."

Peggy looked at her blankly.

"I'm your new neighbor. Didn't the Murphys tell you? I've rented their house for the winter." Prunella gestured with a toss of her head toward a house across the street, a gray Cape Cod with black trim. She looked at the cat hair matted on the front of Peggy's navy sweatshirt. "I see you've already met Holstein. Isn't he a lamb? I just know we're all going to be good friends."

At that moment, Pie, Peggy's little black cat, rubbed against Peggy's ankle. Holstein hissed. Pie bristled, her back arched. The cats began to yowl, an unholy screech that could shatter glass. Buster, Peggy's golden retriever, barked and lunged for Holstein. Peggy grabbed Buster's collar.

Lavinia came through Peggy's kitchen. "PJ, I thought you were coming over for coffee." She stopped short. "I didn't know you had company . . ."

Lavinia glanced at the grandfather clock in Peggy's hallway. ". . . at this hour."

Prunella Post laughed. A whinny-like sound that made Buster bark even louder.

Raising her voice to be heard over the din, Peggy said, "Lavinia Cooper, Prunella Post. She's rented the Murphy house. I'm Peggy Turner."

"Everyone in Cobb's Landing knows who you are, Mayor Turner."

"Peggy, call me Peggy." Over her shoulder, Peggy yelled up the stairs. "Nicky, come and get Buster."

"Never mind, Nicky," yelled Lavinia. "I'll take him, PJ." Lavinia herded a reluctant Buster into the kitchen and out the back door. Buster bounded through the fresh snow, destroying all traces of Peggy's angel.

Prunella Post remained rooted on Peggy's doorstep. "Did someone mention coffee? I could use a cup myself."

"It'll take a minute," said Peggy. "While it's brewing you might want to take Holstein across the street."

"He'll be no trouble here at all, he likes to watch the Weather Channel. I'll put him on your couch."

"I don't think so," said Peggy firmly. "That's Pie's favorite spot. Why don't you take him home, when you get back the coffee will be ready."

"I would," said Prunella, "but there's a small hitch. I don't have the house key. The Murphys told me to get it from you."

"Coffee's here, PJ," said Lavinia, approaching from the kitchen. "I brought the pot over from my house."

"Lovey, can I talk to you for a minute? I think I'm out of milk and sugar."

Peggy steered Lavinia toward the kitchen as Prunella remarked, "Don't bother on my account, I drink it black."

"Lovey," whispered Peggy, "go and call the Murphys from your house. Find out if they rented the house to Mrs. Post and if we're to give her the key. I don't know that woman from Adam and haven't heard anything from the Murphys since they left here in September."

"Good thinking, PJ," whispered Lavinia. Aloud she said, "I'll be right back with the milk and sugar."

"About that coffee," said Prunella, still standing on the doorstep clutching her cat. "And could I trouble you for the use of your bathroom?"

"Just a sec," said Peggy. "I have to put Pie out." She closed the front door, heading up the stairs two at a time to hunt for Pie.

"Mom," said Nicky crossly. "Why is it so noisy? Who is that woman?"

"Go back to sleep, Nicky."

"I'm awake now."

"Sorry, sweetie. Brush your teeth, get dressed, and I'll make your breakfast. Have you seen Pie?"

Nicky shook his head as he ducked into the bathroom.

Peggy found Pie hunched under the bed, fur bristled and stiff like a toilet brush, looking very put out. Peggy closed her bedroom door and went back downstairs where Lavinia waited in the hallway.

"The Murphys didn't answer," said Lavinia. "I left

a message on their answering machine. What do we do now?"

"I'm not giving their key to a stranger," said Peggy. "Prunella Post can stay at Max's inn until this whole mess gets straightened out."

Peggy opened her front door. "You'd better come in." She spread an old towel on the couch. "Put Holstein there." She picked up the remote for the television. "The Weather Channel?"

Prunella nodded and plunked Holstein on the towel. "You can mute the sound. He only likes the pictures. Your bathroom?"

Peggy gestured to a door under the stairs. "The lavatory is right there. I'll be in the kitchen."

As Peggy finished pouring three cups of coffee, she heard a yowl coming from the living room. Then Nicky entered the kitchen. "Mom, there's a strange cat on the sofa."

"Nicky, did you turn off the television?"

Nicky nodded. "You always yell at me for leaving it on when no one's watching it."

Over the cat yowls, Peggy said, "Turn it back on again. The Weather Channel. Mute the sound. Don't ask, Nicky, just do it. I'll explain later."

The yowls subsided. Nicky came back into the kitchen.

"Mom, can we have waffles? It's Saturday."

"Nicky, why don't you have breakfast at our house this morning," said Lavinia. "Chuck's making blueberry pancakes for Charlie."

"And who is this young man?" asked Prunella Post as she entered the kitchen.

"This is my son Nicky," replied Peggy. "Nicky, this is Mrs. Post."

Nicky mumbled a hello in Mrs. Post's direction, then beat feet out the back door, through the gate separating the two yards, and over to the Cooper's kitchen.

Before taking off her coat, Prunella Post reached in the pocket for a pewter pill box, which she placed on Peggy's kitchen table. "My heart medication. I always keep it handy. Just in case."

"Is it for a chronic condition?" asked Lavinia. "What are you taking? I'm asking because I'm a nurse at the county hospital."

"My doctor back home takes care of all my prescriptions," said Prunella with an airy wave of her hand. "I just follow doctor's orders." She began drinking her coffee, then looked around the kitchen. "I don't suppose you have a sliver of toast to go with this?"

It isn't easy to bite your tongue and smile at the same time, but Peggy pulled it off as she reached for a loaf of bread and popped one slice in the toaster.

"What exactly brings you to Cobb's Landing?" asked Lavinia.

"A New England winter, I guess." Prunella shrugged. "I always wanted to spend a winter in a quaint little town like this one."

Peggy grabbed the toasted bread with two fingertips and dropped it onto a plate. She reached for a knife to butter it as Lavinia said, "How do you know Gerald and Sara?"

"Who?" A frown creased Prunella's forehead.

Peggy's hand remained in midair.

"The Murphys," said Lavinia patiently.

"I've never met them in my life," Prunella replied matter-of-factly.

The ensuing silence was broken by the clatter of the stainless steel butter knife hitting Peggy's kitchen floor.

CHAPTER 2

LAVINIA WAS SO MAD SHE WAS SPUTTERING.

"The nerve of that woman, PJ! She invades your house, plops that cow cat on your couch, imposes on you for coffee—and toast for Lord's sake—and she doesn't even *know* the Murphys?"

"I agree, Lovey." Peggy smiled ruefully. "Prunella Post is a piece of work. But if what she says is true about renting through a house-swap agency, we'll get it straightened out. In the meantime, she can cool her heels at Max's inn or Clemmie's Cafe." Peggy grinned at her friend. "If you hadn't been here to back me up, I might not have had the nerve to ask her to leave."

"You've done the same for me in the past, PJ. Remember how you stood up to our third grade teacher when she accused me of hiding her stupid blackboard eraser?" Lavinia giggled as she finished the slice of toast Prunella had hastily abandoned uneaten. "Come on, let's get Chuck to make us some of those blueberry pancakes. I'm famished."

Peggy carefully locked her house—front and back doors—and went with Lavinia into the Cooper's kitchen.

Chuck, Charlie, and Nicky were watching Saturday morning cartoons in the living room, syrup-sticky breakfast plates abandoned on the round oak pedestal table, a match to the table in Peggy's own kitchen.

Peggy began clearing the table while Lavinia whipped up a fresh batch of pancake batter.

Chuck ambled into the kitchen to refill his coffee cup. "I was going to clean up the mess, hon. Honest."

Lavinia rolled her eyes, but smiled affectionately at her husband. "Uh huh."

Chuck put down his cup to answer the phone. "Sara? Sure. Lavinia's right here." He held out the receiver to Lavinia and began pouring batter into the cast-iron skillet. "How many for you, Peggy?"

Peggy held up two fingers as she listened to Lavinia's side of the conversation.

"Really? Paid until March first? So it's okay to give her the key? We'll take care of it, Sara. Right. And our love to you and Gerald. See you next spring."

Lavinia hung up the phone and sat down at the table. "PJ, we've got egg on our faces."

Peggy spewed a mouthful of coffee onto Lavinia's golden oak table. She grabbed a paper napkin to mop up the mess. "How so, Lovey?"

"Dear Sara sent us a letter two weeks ago explaining about the house swap, but she didn't put enough postage on it. The post office returned it to Sara for postage due and she reposted it to us yesterday. Everything Prunella Post said is true."

"Who is Prunella Post?" asked Chuck, setting plates of hot pancakes in front of Lavinia and Peggy.

"I'll give you the condensed version, Chuck," said Lavinia. "Prunella Post is an obnoxious woman with a horrid fat cat who has rented the Murphy's house for the winter. She's going to be our new neighbor."

Chuck, Lavinia, and Peggy sighed unhappily in unison like a Greek chorus.

"PJ, you've got to open the hardware store in less than hour. I'll hunt down Prunella and give her the key. But that's as far as being neighborly goes with me. She's not going to be my new best friend."

"Works for me, Lovey."

The women high-fived before diving into their pancakes.

While Chuck, Charlie, and Nicky were digging in the basement for sleds and saucers for a morning sledding down the hill near the old cemetery, Peggy and Lavinia donned coats, scarves, and mittens for the walk over to Main Street to Tom's Tools and Hardware.

The sky was still overcast, the snow fresh underfoot on the unshovelled sidewalks. As they kicked the snow with their boots, it glistened in the air like sugar-fine silver-white confetti. Overnight, Cobb's Landing had been transformed into a winter wonderland.

"Too bad it'll probably turn to yucky slush by noon," said Peggy, gazing up at the snow-covered tree limbs as she walked.

Lavinia was too busy picking up a mittenful of frosty fluff to reply. She quickly pulled back the collar of Peggy's coat and dropped the snow down Peggy's back. Peggy yelped, grabbed her own handful of snow, and proceeded to wash Lavinia's face. The two women laughed, pelting each other with snow as they ran toward Main Street.

They arrived at Tom's Tools, rosy cheeked and out of breath, to find Prunella Post sitting complacently on the wooden bench outside the front door of the hardware store, moving her legs back and forth under the bench like a kid on a swing set. Holstein was hunched at her side, glowering like a gargoyle.

"Prunella," said Peggy brightly. "I'm glad we found you."

"Here," said Lavinia, handing the key to the Murphys' house to Prunella. "Let's go and get you settled. I'll show you how the furnace works." Shooting Peggy a "You owe me big time" look, Lavinia steered Prunella away from Tom's Tools and back toward the Murphy house.

Holstein hissed at Peggy before leaping off the bench to pad after his mistress.

Peggy made a face at the retreating cat, then went inside Tom's Tools. After moving her supply of snow shovels closer to the front door—where they sold out in an hour—Peggy began pulling stock for her Thanksgiving display window.

Saturday mornings were always a busy time at

Tom's Tools. Slim, Bob, and the gang of guys who made a ritual of Saturday breakfast at Clemmie's Cafe came to Tom's Tools to hang out, cadge a cup of post-breakfast coffee, and dispense free advice to the do-it-yourselfers engaged in weekend projects.

Lavinia popped in about noon as the Clemmie's gang was leaving. "I went sledding with Chuck and the boys. Whee! PJ, I haven't had that much fun on a sled since we were kids. Snow's still holding and the boys want to go sledding again after lunch. Can you close early and come with us? Chuck's going to Bob's to spend the afternoon watching football."

Peggy looked at the wall clock. "I'll meet you at the hill at about two. I want to finish my store window before I leave. Tell Nicky to get my saucer out of our basement."

Lavinia laughed. "Nicky's been using it all morning. Still works great. I'm going home to give the guys soup and grilled cheese sandwiches for lunch. How about we all have pizza tonight? Your treat. You owe me for this morning." Lavinia grinned wickedly as she beat a hasty retreat out of Tom's Tools.

Peggy went back to her store window. Using nylon fishing line suspended from the ceiling, she created an Alexander Calder mobile effect with kitchen cooking implements associated with Thanksgiving. The centerpiece was a blue enameled roaster like the one that had belonged to Peggy's grandmother. Flanking it were turkey skewers for keeping the stuffing inside the bird, pastry brushes, basting tubes, slotted spoons, gravy ladles, and an old-fashioned hand grinder that every New Englander knew was the only way to make really good cranberry-orange relish. For a backdrop Peggy used colored markers to sketch on white butcher paper a running turkey being chased by a pilgrim.

As she turned to grab the hammer and tacks from the counter to fasten the backdrop in place, Peggy was surprised—and mildly irritated—to find Max standing behind her quietly eyeing the window display, his right elbow cupped in his left hand, fingers of his right hand tapping his chin. Max's pose reminded Peggy of old photos of Jack Benny. As usual, Max was attired in a suit, this one a navy pinstripe, accented with his trademark red silk bow tie.

"Max! How do you keep doing that?"

"Doing what?" A grin lit Max's elfin face. "Are you accusing me of skulking? Moi?"

Peggy sighed—Max could be so infuriating. She tacked the backdrop top and bottom, then closed the plywood window backing. There were some questions to which Max would never give straight answers; his sudden comings and goings would always be a mystery Peggy was itching to solve.

Peggy put the hammer and tacks in the counter drawer. "What brings you out today, Max? Fleecing widows and orphans? Bilking tourists?"

Max made a tsking sound with his tongue against the back of his upper teeth. "I'm shocked, Mayor. Shocked that you would accuse me of such nefariosity."

Peggy looked at Max. "Nefari what? Is that a real word?"

"If it isn't, it should be." Max paused. "Actually

I've come to beg a boon of thee and do thee a good turn as recompense."

"Max, speak English will you? What do you want?"

As Max started to reply, he was drowned out by a voice Peggy was quickly coming to loathe more than the sound of fingernails screeching down a chalkboard.

"Whose cute little horse-drawn sleigh is that outside? I would just love a ride in something like that."

"My good woman," Max boomed sternly, "whoever you may be, you have ruined my surprise. Be gone with you."

Peggy rolled her eyes. "Max, meet Prunella Post. She's rented the Murphy house for the winter. Prunella, this is Max. He owns our local bank and the inn on the river."

There was a lot more Peggy could have added to that brief introduction. How Max had suddenly appeared in Cobb's Landing about nine months earlier with a plan to turn the town into a colonial-themed tourist attraction, Colonial Village—a plan that had saved Peggy's beloved hometown from economic disaster. She also could have added that she wasn't sure if Max was a guardian angel or the devil incarnate or an escapee from a lunatic asylum or merely an eccentric elderly rich man; but whatever he was, life was seldom dull when Max was about. Even if Peggy felt like strangling Max most of the time, on the whole she'd become rather fond of him. Those were things she could have added, but didn't. One thing Peggy knew for sure, as irritating as Max could be, he didn't hold a candle to Prunella Post when it came to winning the Pain In The Tush award. In the few short hours she'd been in Cobb's Landing, Prunella had retired the PITT trophy. No contest.

Max acknowledged the introduction with a flicking gesture of his right hand toward Prunella. "Shoo. Shoo. Shoo. I have business to discuss with the mayor, and you have rudely interrupted me."

Prunella scurried out the door of Tom's Tools as if she'd been repeatedly zapped by a cattle prod while Peggy stared in astonishment.

"Max, I don't know what you just did, but whatever favor you want, ask away. I've been trying to get rid of that woman all morning, but she keeps turning up like a bad penny."

"You leave her to me. Pesky people always get what they deserve. You'll see." Max held out his arm to Peggy. "It's time you closed for the day. Shall we take a ride?"

"I'm supposed to meet Nicky at the sledding hill."

"I'll be glad to drop you there. We can talk as we go."

CHAPTER 3

THE SNOWFALL HADN'T BEEN DEEP ENOUGH TO warrant either plowing or the added expense to the perpetually sliding-into-the-red Cobb's Landing town budget, so Main Street was still covered with snow that was becoming hard-packed by traffic.

Outside Tom's Tools a one-horse open sleigh was parked, reminding Peggy of the traditional Thanksgiving song "Over the River and Through the Woods." When Peggy was comfortably seated in the fire-engine-red sleigh—naturally Max *would* choose a red one—Max picked up the reins and clucked softly to the coal black horse. Soon they were slowly gliding along Main Street, heading for the sliding hill near the old cemetery on the far edge of town.

As the elevation increased, Peggy turned to look behind her at the snow-covered roofs, thin curls of smoke rising from chimneys, and finally the old red brick button factory—now Max's bed-and-break-fast—nestled on the bank of the Rock River.

"You're not paying attention," Max chided. "I'm talking and you're not listening."

"Sorry, Max. I was just enjoying the view. You were saying . . . ?"

"I was saying that sleighs would be the ideal transport for our Thanksgiving visitors."

"The weather can be very iffy this time of year, Max. Snow today, slush tonight, back to bare ground in less than a day."

"You leave the weather to me," said Max. "If I want snow, there'll *be* snow. Although it's not my natural element. I prefer things, shall we say, a little more toasty."

Peggy smiled as Max continued. "You like the sleigh idea? They'll be bigger than this one of course."

"The sleighs are wonderful, Max."

"We could charge extra for the ride, or make it part of the dinner package. What do you think?"

"Max, get to the point. What are you talking about?"

"Thanksgiving, of course."

"Thanksgiving?"

Max turned to stare at Peggy. "Are you having a memory lapse? Perhaps you need more vitamins. May I suggest ginkgo biloba? Stimulates blood flow to the brain. Does wonders for the memory. I'll send you some."

"Max, there's nothing wrong with my memory."

"Then you do remember my saying about a week

ago that I want to have a reenactment of the first
Thanksgiving dinner here in Cobb's Landing. I've already put it on the Colonial Village Web site, and the
reservations are pouring in. We'll limit the seating,
make it fairly exclusive. Say two hundred guests,
tops? We should be able to fit that many on the village green. Long tables, of course, serve everyone
family style. Hmmmm. Perhaps a buffet at the inn
would be better. About the menu—turkey of
course."

"Max, here's a mini-flash for you. There was no
turkey served at the first Thanksgiving in Cobb's
Landing."

"How do you know?"

"I looked it up in the town records. The first
Thanksgiving in Cobb's Landing was held in November, 1863 when it was declared a national holiday by President Lincoln."

"You sure it was 1863?"

"Positive, Max. And it wasn't on the town green
either. There was over a foot of snow on the ground
and the temperature was way below freezing."

"All right, little Miss know-it-all, where was this
sumptuous feast held?"

"At the old church at the cemetery. The one that
was destroyed by lightning. It was the only place at
the time that had enough room to seat everyone."

The word *church* hit Max like a wooden stake
through his heart. "All right. Enough local trivia. I
want to know what they ate."

"Eels."

"Eels?"

"Eels, Max. They ate eels."

"Hmmmmm." Max thought for a moment. "Tasty for an appetizer. I had it at an Explorer's Club dinner. I would have preferred smoked rattlesnake. That tastes like chicken. But spicier."

"There's no accounting for taste, Max."

Max ignored Peggy's retort. "And what other gourmet fare did the colonials consume, pray tell?"

"Corn, squash, turnips, and some sort of pumpkin-apple-cranberry compote."

"Not very festive. I'm sure we can come up with something better," said Max. "I'll put you in charge of the menu."

"Max, I never dreamed you were serious about Thanksgiving. I thought we agreed months ago that Colonial Village closed November first. Everyone's put their costumes away until next spring."

"Well, they can just get them out again. This is a money-making opportunity we can't afford to pass up."

"Oh Max, not Thanksgiving."

"And why not?" Max pulled the reins and the horse stopped in its tracks.

"Because Thanksgiving is my favorite holiday, and I'm not going to share it with a bunch of tourists. That's why not." Peggy folded her arms and nodded emphatically. "Thanksgiving is a family day. I want to spend it in my own house with only people I know and love."

Max's slit-eyed stare reminded Peggy of Holstein. "Is that your final word on the subject?"

"Yes, Max, it is."

"We'll see about that." Max motioned to Peggy to get out of the sleigh with the same abrupt shooing gesture he'd used on Prunella Post. "I think you can walk to the sledding hill from here; it's only a few yards away."

Peggy took a few steps, then turned to look back. Max and the sleigh were nowhere to be seen.

"Hey, Mom, we're over here!" Nicky called to Peggy from the bottom of the hill.

Peggy and Lavinia spent the rest of the afternoon sledding with Nicky and Charlie. They took turns using the sleds and saucers that had belonged to the two women when they were eleven, sliding down the very same hill.

On the way home, they stopped at Alsop's Bakery to pick up the pizzas Peggy had ordered. Charlie and Nicky tried to be nonchalant, but both Peggy and Lavinia knew the boys were looking for Maria, the pretty little dark-haired daughter of Gina and Lew Alsop. It was no secret that both Nicky and Charlie had big crushes on Maria.

"Maria just went home with her mother," said Lew, repressing a smile. "I'll tell them you all were here." As he handed Peggy her change, Lew added, "Max stopped by this afternoon. He wants the bakery to make all the bread and pies for the Thanksgiving feast. He's paying top dollar, too. Sure can't turn down a deal like that."

Peggy made polite responses while inwardly grimacing. She knew Max well enough to know he was single-minded when it came to getting what he wanted, but she'd be damned if she was going to give in to Max on something as important to her as Thanksgiving.

Juggling the hot pizza boxes, Peggy fished in her jacket pocket for her keys as she approached her front door. Sitting in front of the door was Holstein.

"Nicky, I need you to hold the pizza boxes. Keep them away from that damned cat."

Prunella approached from across the street. "Have you seen Holstein? Oh, there he is. Come here, you naughty kitty." Holstein didn't budge an inch. Prunella sniffed the air. "Pizza? Do I smell pizza? Just the ticket for a nippy Saturday night. Hope you didn't order anchovies. I personally hate them, although Holstein thinks they're a treat. He picks them off with his paw. Isn't he cute?"

Peggy was determined to quell any thoughts Prunella was having about horning in on Peggy's Saturday night.

"Prunella," Peggy said firmly. "You can get your own pizza at Alsop's Bakery on Main Street. If you hurry, you can get there before they shut down the ovens. I'd go now if I were you. Gotta go, I hear my phone ringing."

"I don't hear anything," said Prunella.

Peggy edged Holstein aside with the toe of her boot, opened her front door, and motioned Nicky inside.

"Have a nice night." Peggy slipped into her house, closed the door, then leaned back against it, exhaling a sigh of relief.

Outside, Holstein howled.

CHAPTER 4

THE PIZZA WAS HISTORY, REDUCED TO ERRANT crust fragments in the now cold cardboard boxes.

Nicky and Charlie had gone into the living room to watch a zombie film fest on the Sci-Fi Channel.

"How many times can those boys watch *Night of the Living Dead*? They already know most of the dialogue by heart," said Lavinia, laughing. She sucked air from her beer bottle. "Is there any beer left, Chuck?"

Chuck fetched three well-chilled beers from Peggy's refrigerator and put them on the kitchen table.

Peggy had just taken a healthy swig of her beer when the phone rang. Chuck motioned that he'd answer it.

"Stu? Hey, man, where are you? Yeah, this is Chuck. You called the right number, we're at

Peggy's. We just finished eating pizza. Wait a minute, I'll put Peggy on." Chuck handed the receiver to Peggy.

"Hey, Stu. We're all so glad you're coming back to Cobb's Landing. Your old job is waiting. When can we expect you? I know your mother will be happy to have you home again." As Peggy listened to Stu, the expression on her face segued from a broad smile to incredulous and finally to mildly annoyed. "I really don't want to do this, Stu. It's asking quite a lot. Why can't you tell her yourself?" Peggy listened again, reaching for her beer bottle for another healthy swallow. "Don't try to sweet-talk me, Stu. I've known you far too long. All right, all right. I'll do it. Yes, I'll do it tomorrow. Don't thank me yet because I haven't done anything. But remember this, you owe me big time and forever. We'll talk more when you get here. Bye Stu. See you soon. Drive safely." Peggy hung up the phone and sat slowly shaking her head.

"What was all that about?" asked Lavinia.

"You're not going to believe this," said Peggy. "Stu expects to be back early next week, but he's not coming home alone. He's bringing his fiancée with him and wants me to break the news to his mother."

Lavinia: "Sheesh."

Chuck: "Stu, you sly dog!"

Peggy sat drinking her beer, idly drumming her fingertips on the tabletop. "Damn. I can't believe he asked me to do that."

Lavinia chuckled. "I can't believe you agreed to it."

Chuck yawned and stretched. "I can't believe Stu hasn't broken free of his mother before this. He's our age, for Pete's sake. It's about time he declared his independence from that domineering witch. If she was my mother, I would have left home the second I learned how to crawl." Chuck picked up his beer and headed for the living room. "I'll let you two hash it out. I'd rather watch *Night of the Living Dead*. Dealing with zombies is a picnic compared to Stu's mother."

Lavinia leaned toward Peggy. "Details, PJ. Give me all the dirt about Stu's new fiancée. What's her name?"

Peggy shrugged. "I was so surprised, I didn't even think to ask. And I never offered my congratulations."

"When are you going to break the news to old Mrs. McIntyre?"

"The sooner the better, Lovey. I'd call her now but it's too late and the sound of her shrieks would give me nightmares."

Lavinia laughed. "Let's hope old Mrs. McIntyre doesn't decide to shoot the messenger."

"I don't suppose you'd . . ."

"Not on your life, PJ. I love you more than a sister, but that's asking too much. Besides, I dealt with Prunella Post this morning."

"You did not. We both did, outside the hardware store."

"Yes, but I took her to the Murphys' house and spent half an hour listening to her prattle. You owe me for that one."

"Oh, very well," Peggy grumbled. "But you don't have to rub it in."

"Why didn't Ian join us for pizza? I thought you two had a date tonight," said Lavinia.

"He called just after I got home. Something about a last-minute meeting with Max he couldn't get out of."

"Hmmmmm," said Lavinia. "Sounds a little suspect to me. You buying that story?"

"Max is annoyed with me," said Peggy. "I think he was getting back at me for this afternoon."

"Why?"

"Because I'm not going along with his plans for a colonial Thanksgiving feast to rake in tourist dollars."

"I didn't think Max was serious. It's a dumb idea," said Lavinia. "Someone needs to clue Max in about Thanksgiving in Cobb's Landing. Everyone watches the Macy's parade on television, then we eat a big turkey dinner, later the guys all fall asleep watching football. It's tradition."

"You tell Max. I tried and failed miserably. I even told him about the eels."

"What eels?"

"They ate eels at the first Thanksgiving in Cobb's Landing. I looked it up."

Lavinia made an ugly face. "Eels? How revolting."

"Max says they make a good appetizer, but he prefers smoked rattlesnake."

"He would. Although I didn't think snakes devoured their own."

Peggy reached for a pad and pen. "Let's make out our Thanksgiving list. I want to shop tomorrow afternoon while we can still get everything. Don't forget, dinner's at my house this year."

"Chuck had a great idea about the turkey. He saw a segment on deep-frying turkeys on the Food Channel and has been talking about doing one that way ever since. What do you think?"

"Sounds great, Lovey, but I'll roast a backup bird, just in case. You can't have too many leftovers."

"Good plan, PJ. What else are we going to have?"

"The usual, I suppose."

"I'll make a sweet potato casserole topped with mini-marshmallows. The boys love that."

"I'll do the mashed potatoes and gravy."

Lavinia giggled. "Our special gravy? The old family recipe?"

Peggy laughed. "Gravy made with turkey droppings."

"How old were we then, PJ?"

"Five or six?"

"Your dad got a little tiddly and said he was making gravy with turkey droppings. He really meant drippings."

"Remember how annoyed your mother got when we couldn't stop giggling and kept whispering 'turkey droppings, turkey droppings' during grace before dinner?"

The two women smiled at the childhood memory, one of thousands that wove through their friendship and had bonded them like sisters since they were small children.

"What else are we going to have, PJ?"

"Green bean casserole, cranberry-orange relish."

"Dessert? I'll bake my apple mince pie."

"I'll make my frozen pumpkin ice cream pie."

Peggy finished the shopping list and handed it to Lavinia.

"Looks good, PJ. We're going to have another wonderful Thanksgiving. I can hardly wait."

CHAPTER 5

SUNDAY MORNING, PEGGY ROSE AT DAWN AND quickly dressed. The best time to catch old Mrs. McIntyre was on her morning stroll with Poopsie, her rugrat ankle-biting yappy dog. Privately, Peggy referred to old Mrs. McIntyre's morning walk as the dawn patrol, a convenient excuse for snooping on her neighbors.

Peggy whistled for Buster, clipped on his leash, and set out to take her golden retriever for a walk.

The temperature had warmed to slightly above freezing, reducing the once glorious snow to crusty patches on lawns. The air was still, laced with a hint of bone-chilling fog. Peggy felt the damp of the wet concrete sidewalk seep through the soles of her boots and wished she'd worn her thick-soled running shoes. Too late to go back and change. She picked up the pace to keep the blood circulating in her slowly numbing toes. Buster trotted happily alongside, stopping occasionally to sniff a tree or leave his own mark—the canine equivalent of writing his name in the snow.

Main Street was devoid of traffic or human presence, even Clemmie's Cafe was still dark and would remain so for another hour. Peggy turned left toward the circular horse trough that had been a Cobb's Landing fixture for longer than anyone could remember. When Peggy reached the village green—originally the common where livestock grazed in Josiah Cobb's time—she released Buster from his leash and watched as he joyously romped across the grass like a racehorse doing short sprints. She knew this was in violation of the leash law, but if someone complained she'd pay the fine.

Peggy spotted old Mrs. McIntyre approaching from the far side of the green, Poopsie straining at the leash. Peggy waved, took a deep breath, and walked toward Stu's mother.

The morning calm was broken by a shrill "yoo hoo" coming from the area of the horse trough and the blur of a black and white cat hell-bent on a kamikaze suicide mission.

Peggy dropped her own leash as she accelerated from zero to sixty in under five seconds. But she was too late. Holstein had found his target.

Between Poopsic's yowls, Holstein's howls, Buster's barks, old Mrs. McIntyre's shrieks, and Prunella Post's whinny-like wails, Peggy could hardly hear herself think.

"Buster, stay!"

Buster reluctantly stayed.

Poopsie's leash had wound around old Mrs. McIntyre's ankles, causing her to lose her footing and fall face down in the remnants of snow.

"Prunella, call off your damned cat."

Prunella Post continued to wail and cling to the horse trough for support.

Peggy plunged into the fray.

Once Holstein and Poopsie were separated—and Holstein plopped unceremoniously into Prunella's arms with a stern warning from Peggy about obeying the Cobb's Landing leash law—Peggy helped old Mrs. McIntyre to her feet.

Poopsie lay panting and whimpering, drops of blood from the gashes on his head staining the snow crimson.

Now it was old Mrs. McIntyre's turn to wail.

"Everything will be okay," said Peggy. "Give me five minutes to run home and get my car and we'll take Poopsie to the vet."

Peggy wrapped Poopsie in an old but clean bath towel and placed the little dog gently into Mrs. McIntyre's lap. "I called the vet. Doctor Lewis is expecting us."

After Poopsie's wounds had been disinfected, stitched, and the little dog pumped full of antibiotics, Peggy drove old Mrs. McIntyre home.

"Do you want me to come back tomorrow morning?" asked Peggy as she walked old Mrs. McIntyre to her front door. "Doctor Lewis said you could pick up Poopsie tomorrow after ten."

"That's quite all right," said old Mrs. McIntyre with

a small martyred sigh. "I'll manage. You've done more than enough. If only Stu were here, I'd have him arrest that horrid woman and her beastly cat."

Here was the opening Peggy wanted, but did she have the courage to run with it? She took a deep breath. "About Stu. He called me last night."

"Why would he call you and not his own mother?"

"Was your phone out of order?" Peggy could feel her nose beginning to grow as she added, "Stu said he tried calling you, but couldn't get through."

"I'll have the phone checked immediately."

"Stu told me he'd be back in Cobb's Landing in a few days. Lavinia and I want to have a welcome home party for Stu and his fiancée. What day do you think would be good?"

"Fiancée? What fiancée?" A vein began to throb in old Mrs. McIntyre's neck.

"I didn't get her name. I assumed you knew," said Peggy, telling another bald-faced lie. "You look a little peaky. You've had an unsettling morning. A nice cup of tea and little nap will fix you right up. I'll call later—if your phone is working—to check on you."

Mission accomplished, Peggy fled to the sanctuary of her car and headed for home. She parked on the street, in front of the Murphys' house, then went into her own house for a cat carrier and back across the street to knock on the Murphys' front door. "Open up, Prunella, I know you're in there." Peggy saw a hand pull back the curtain and caught a fleeting glimpse of Prunella's face in the window. She knocked again.

Prunella answered the front door. "My, my. What a nice surprise. You're my first caller."

"Prunella, this isn't a social visit." Peggy handed Prunella the cat carrier. "I want you to put Holstein in this carrier and we're taking him to the vet. Now. He needs to be quarantined and tested for rabies."

"I won't do it." Prunella stuck out her chin defiantly.

"Oh yes, you will," said Peggy. "This isn't a request, it's an order. I'm not only the mayor of Cobb's Landing, but also the temporary police chief. Are you going to get that cat or am I?"

Wrestling Holstein into the cat carrier was worse than trying to stuff a twenty-pound live octopus into a ten-pound container.

When Holstein was confined and yowling in the carrier, Peggy mopped the sweat from her brow. "Do you have Holstein's vet records? Doctor Lewis will want to see them."

Prunella hesitated. "I didn't bring them with me."

"Fine," said Peggy. "Get your coat. You can give Claudia Lewis all the details and she'll get the records faxed to her."

Prunella was uncommonly silent during the short ride to Claudia's office. But Holstein made up for his mistress' silence by moaning, shrieking, and howling all the way.

Claudia Lewis was brisk and professional. "I'll get in touch with your vet in . . ." Claudia looked at her clipboard, ". . . Fostoria, Ohio. If Holstein's rabies shots are current I'll be able to release him tomorrow. Otherwise, I'll have to hold him for observation here at the clinic for ten days."

Prunella's shrieks were far more ear shattering than Holstein's.

Peggy thanked Claudia and hustled Prunella out of the clinic.

"You have no one to blame but yourself, Prunella," said Peggy, her patience wearing thin. "You brought that cat to a strange town without his medical papers and you've let him run loose in a village with a leash law."

Prunella stubbornly declined a ride, saying she wanted fresh air and would walk home.

When Peggy got into her car, she quickly discovered why Prunella had opted to walk. One sniff told Peggy that Holstein had peed all over the back seat.

CHAPTER 6

AFTER STOPPING AT TOM'S TOOLS FOR EVERY cleaning agent she could get her hands on to scrub the back seat, then thoroughly disinfecting her car with two cans of Lysol spray, Peggy went home and into her kitchen for a much needed cup of coffee.

Propped on the table was a note from Lavinia. *Nicky's at our house. Chuck's making kitchen sink scrambled eggs. I took the bacon from your fridge. Come over for breakfast as soon as you read this.*

The coffee was almost ready when Peggy's phone rang.

"Peggy, it's Claudia Lewis. Sorry to bother you, but I need your help. Can you come back to the clinic right away?"

"Coffee, Claudia. I haven't had any coffee. I need lots of it. Now. I've been too busy getting the stink of cat pee out of the back seat of my car."

Peggy heard Claudia's low and husky laugh. "I've got a home remedy for cat pee stink, and there's lots of hot coffee ready and waiting. Please hurry, Peggy."

For the third time—and she hoped the last time of the morning—Peggy headed for Claudia's animal clinic. Although she drove with all the windows open, Peggy could still smell Holstein.

The clinic was located in a small annex—formerly a two-car garage—attached to Claudia's two-story frame house. The house and annex were painted a bright buttercup yellow with charcoal gray trim. A discreet brass plaque on the annex entrance was engraved *Claudia Lewis, Veterinarian.*

When Peggy entered Claudia's waiting room, she immediately saw the reason for Claudia's frantic S.O.S. Seated in a hard plastic chair was Prunella Post, face like thundercloud under her orange knit hat, arms tightly folded across the front of her mud-brown down coat.

The sight of Prunella curdled any remaining milk of human kindness into a sour mass in the pit of Peggy's stomach. "Prunella, enough. I want you to go home immediately."

"I'm not leaving here without Holstein." Prunella remained glued to the plastic chair.

Peggy took a deep breath and addressed Prunella in calm, even tones. "You have been in Cobb's Landing only twenty-four hours. In that time you have managed to alienate everyone you've met. I was prepared to welcome you because I am very fond of Gerald and Sara Murphy and want to please their tenants, but you have tried my patience to the limit."

Claudia handed Peggy a cup of coffee.

"By the time I've finished this coffee, I want you out of Claudia's clinic. It's Sunday. A day of rest. For everyone. Including you."

"But what am I going to do?" Prunella wailed.

All of her life Peggy had been waiting for the opportunity to use a classic line from one of her favorite movies. The time had finally come.

" 'Frankly, my dear, I don't give a damn.' "

Prunella Post scurried out of Claudia's waiting room without a backward glance.

"Way to go, Peggy." Claudia applauded. "How about a refill on that coffee?"

"Claudia, have you had breakfast? Chuck Cooper is making his famous kitchen sink scrambled eggs and he always makes way too much. C'mon, let's go."

Claudia and Peggy walked into the Cooper's kitchen to find Chuck, Lavinia, Charlie, and Nicky ready to attack mounds of scrambled eggs and bacon. Lavinia quickly grabbed two extra plates and motioned to the boys to move over and make room at the table.

"Claudia, it's always great to see you. I'm glad you're here" said Lavinia. "Where have you been, PJ? You've been gone for hours."

"Don't ask until after I've eaten," replied Peggy between hearty swigs of coffee. "You don't want to hear about it on an empty stomach."

"These eggs smell great," said Claudia, fork in hand poised over her plate. "What's in them?"

"Everything but the kitchen sink," said Chuck

with a grin. "It's my variation of the garbage omelet. Whatever bits and dabs I find in the refrigerator, I dice, sauté, and mix in with the eggs. They're never the same twice."

"Mom," said Nicky, pushing his empty plate aside. "What am I going to do today? I wanted to go sledding, but the snow is almost gone."

"I've got a great idea," said Peggy. "We're all going to the mall. Lavinia and I are getting our Thanksgiving shopping done."

"Bor-ring, Mom."

"Wait, Nicky. You haven't heard the best part." Peggy ruffled her son's hair, a gesture eleven-year-old Nicky barely tolerated. Geez. He wasn't a kid anymore. "While we shop, you and Charlie can go to a movie."

"Really, Mom?" said Charlie.

Lavinia smiled and nodded.

"Cool." A big grin lit Charlie's face.

"You want to go with us, Chuck?" asked Lavinia.

"On a football Sunday?" Chuck smiled, shaking his head. "I'll clean up the kitchen: you guys go and have fun. I'll make a big pot of chili for dinner."

"Only one catch, Lovey," said Peggy. "You have to drive."

"Sure, no problem," said Lavinia. "Is something wrong with your car?"

"Holstein peed all over the back seat this morning."

"Eeeeeew. Mom, that's gross," said Nicky.

"Yeah, Nicky, it *is* gross, and worse than that, it still stinks."

"Can we get a new car?"

"No, Nicky, we cannot get a new car."

"I'll help you get rid of that smell," said Claudia. "We need white vinegar and baking soda."

After scrubbing the back seat with a solution of white vinegar and water, open boxes of baking soda were placed in the car to absorb any remaining odor.

"That should do it, Peggy. I also recommend using orange oil. Cats hate the citrus scent," said Claudia. "Thanks for coming to my rescue with Mrs. Post and inviting me to breakfast. I'll call you as soon as I've heard from the vet in Ohio."

While Nicky and Charlie went to see the newest Harry Potter movie, Peggy and Lavinia pushed a cart through the discount grocery store. In addition to Peggy's Thanksgiving shopping list, Chuck had a few additions of his own for his Cajun deep-fried turkey.

"When did Chuck develop this interest in cooking?" asked Peggy.

"When he's not watching sports, he's glued to the Food Channel," said Lavinia. "I'm glad he wants to cook. Saves me from hearing those dreaded three little words—'What's for dinner?'—every night."

Peggy smiled. "I'll push the cart, you pile in the groceries."

While they waited in the checkout line, Lavinia said, "Tell me what Holstein was doing in your car this morning."

Peggy related the whole story, beginning with meeting old Mrs. McIntyre on the village green.

Lavinia doubled over with laughter. "I wish I'd

been there. It sounds like one of those monster-meets-monster sci-fi movies the boys love."

"*Godzilla vs. Mothra*?" Peggy giggled.

Lavinia smiled. "Did you ever get around to telling old Mrs. Mac about Stu and his fiancée?"

Peggy nodded. "I did, but I wasn't at my diplomatic best about it. I sort of angled it into the conversation after I took her home from Claudia's clinic. And I'm afraid I put us on the hook as well."

"How?"

"I said you and I wanted to have a party for Stu and his fiancée."

"Great idea, PJ. Wait right here."

"Where are you going, Lovey?"

"To grab another turkey. Chuck can practice his deep-frying skills on Stu before he does the bird for Thanksgiving."

CHAPTER 7

IF PEGGY THOUGHT SHE'D SEEN THE LAST OF
Prunella Post, she was dead wrong.

No sooner had Peggy opened Tom's Tools on
Monday morning, let Pie out of her carrier, and
started a pot of coffee, when Prunella sailed into the
hardware store as if she owned the place.

"Show me where to hang my coat, I'm ready to go
to work."

Peggy wasn't fazed by much, but this brazen as-
sumption knocked her for a loop.

"Prunella, what are you talking about? I don't
need help."

"Of course you do. I'm not asking you to pay me.
I just thought I'd help out here a few hours a day."

Peggy felt as if a really big camel, one the size of
the beast that ate Cleveland, had just stuck its nose
into her tent.

"No. Absolutely not."

Prunella was caught with her coat half on, half off, one arm still in the sleeve, orange knit cap still on her head. "No?"

"No," Peggy said firmly.

At that moment, the phone rang. Saved, Peggy thought as she grabbed the receiver. "Tom's Tools." She listened for a moment. "Oh, that is good news. She's right here. I'll tell her. Thanks, Claudia."

"Prunella, that was Claudia Lewis. Holstein's vet records came and he's in the clear. You can pick him up at the clinic and take him home."

With Prunella once again out of her hair, Peggy went to the urn to pour a much needed cup of coffee.

The door of Tom's Tools opened, letting in a gust of air that chilled the back of Peggy's neck. Then a pair of arms wrapped around her from behind, enveloping her in a warm bear hug. A voice in her ear said, "Got a cup of coffee for an old friend?"

Peggy looked up to see Stu McIntyre grinning down at her. She turned and gave Stu a kiss on the cheek and a big hug. "Oh, Stu. Welcome home! I didn't think you'd get here so soon." Then Peggy noticed a pretty blonde woman about her own age, dressed in a forest-green loden coat, standing quietly a few feet away. "Stu, aren't you going to introduce us?"

A faint blush added more color to Stu's cheeks, already ruddy from the cold outside air. "Peggy, this is Emily. My fiancée."

Peggy clasped Emily's hand in hers. "I'm so glad to meet you. Welcome to Cobb's Landing."

The door to Tom's Tools opened again. "PJ, is the coffee ready yet? I brought cranberry muffins." Lavinia stopped in her tracks, dropped the sack of muffins on the checkout counter, then ran to give Stu a welcome home hug.

"Lovey, this is Emily, Stu's fiancée. Emily, this is Lavinia Cooper." Peggy turned to Emily. "I'm sorry, I don't know your last name."

"Post. Emily Post."

"Post?" said Peggy. "Like the good manners Emily Post?"

"No relation, I'm afraid," replied Emily with a small smile. "I'm from Ohio."

"My God," said Lavinia. "Just like Prunella."

"Who?" Emily blanched, her pink cheeks paled to ghost white. "Did you say Prunella?"

Lavinia nodded briskly. "Prunella Post. She came here last weekend from someplace in Ohio. She's spending the winter in Cobb's Landing."

Emily slowly collapsed into a faint onto the planked wood floor of Tom's Tools.

CHAPTER 8

IN HER YEARS AS A NURSE, LAVINIA HAD DEALT with many fainters; including, on one memorable occasion, her best friend Peggy when a body was discovered on the water wheel at the old button factory. In a matter of seconds, Lavinia had Emily seated in a straight-backed chair, coat unbuttoned, head between her knees.

"PJ, can you rustle up a cup of hot tea? With lots of sugar?"

When Emily had revived, normal color back in her cheeks and was sipping the hot tea, Peggy queried gently, "Do you know Prunella Post?"

Emily nodded, then shook her head. "We're related. We were. I mean we're not anymore. She is, I mean she was, my mother-in-law."

Stu looked at Emily in surprise. "You were married before?"

Lowering her chin and giving Stu a shy-Di look under the lashes of her big blue eyes, Emily whispered "yes" then went back to sipping her tea.

"When were you planning on telling me?" asked Stu.

Peggy motioned to Lavinia. "Lovey, come outside and take a look at my display window. Tell me what you think of it."

When the two women were outside, Lavinia still warm in her coat while Peggy was feeling the chill through her turtleneck and sweater, Peggy said, "I thought Stu and Emily needed a moment without us."

"Oh Lord," said Lavinia, "I hope Stu hasn't messed up again. He's such a bad judge of character when it comes to women."

"Emily seems nice enough."

"PJ, don't be a blithering idiot. You met Emily—what?—five minutes ago? For all you know, she could be an ax murderer." Lavinia opened her coat and wrapped part of it around Peggy. "Let's look at this store window of yours so we're not total liars."

They gazed at the window for an obligatory five seconds.

"Great window, PJ." Lavinia looked closer at the cooking utensils slowly twirling in the light. "Amazing how different ordinary kitchen items look when they're out of the drawer. I'm sure glad I'm not a turkey. I'd hate to be stabbed and trussed with one of those skewers. Let's go back inside. I'm starting to feel the cold."

The outside chill had pervaded the interior of
Tom's Tools. Stu and Emily were standing awk-
wardly apart, not saying anything.

Peggy attempted to bridge the gap between the
sweethearts. "Stu, you must have driven all night to
get here so quickly. I'll bet Emily's tired and could
use a nap. Where are you staying?"

"I've made reservations at Max's inn until we find
a house to rent," replied Stu. "Peggy, could I talk to
you for a minute?"

When Lavinia and Emily were out of earshot, Stu
said quietly, "Did you have a chance to talk to my
mother?"

"Stu," hissed Peggy, "you and I will talk about
this later, but the answer is yes. I talked to your
mother. She knows you're bringing your fiancée
home with you. She also thinks Lavinia and I are
having a welcome home/engagement party for you.
You'd better bring Emily over to my house for dinner tonight so we can make plans for the party."

Stu kissed Peggy on the cheek. "Thanks, Peggy. I
knew I could count on you."

"Don't ever ask me to do that again, Stu. I mean
it. Next time you deal with your mother yourself.
You owe me big time for this."

"I won't forget, Peggy."

"Go on, take Emily to the inn. I'll see you tonight
at my house about six thirty. Okay?"

"Okay."

"Stu?"

"Yes?"

"Before you get all out of sorts about Emily's

marital past, have you told her about your own? Because if you haven't, I will."

The look on Stu's face told Peggy all she needed to know.

When Stu and Emily had left Tom's Tools, Peggy poured coffee for herself and Lavinia, then opened the bag of cranberry muffins.

"What was all that whispering with Stu about?" asked Lavinia.

"He wanted to know if I'd talked to his mother about Emily. I told him I had, but never again. Oh, I also invited Stu and Emily over for dinner tonight, so we can plan the welcome home party. You and Chuck and Charlie had better come, too. Six thirty?"

"Sounds good to me, PJ. Another night I don't have to cook. What are you having?"

Peggy thought for a minute. "Chicken and dumplings, I guess. If I run home now, I can put the chicken in the crockpot and it'll be done by six."

"I'll bring a salad and dessert." Lavinia glanced at the wall clock, an antique Burpee's seed clock with a moon phase dial. "I'm going to be late for my shift at the hospital. See you tonight, PJ."

Peggy put a *Back in 5 Minutes* sign on the door of Tom's Tools and ran home to start dinner. She returned to the hardware store slightly out of breath to find Ian looking at her window display.

"Peggy, we've got to talk," said Ian, bending to brush her cheek with a kiss.

"Are you free for dinner tonight? Stu's back, and the Cooper's are coming."

"Let's go inside," said Ian. "I've only got a minute."

"Oh." Peggy took a good look at Ian. He was dressed in a charcoal gray three-piece suit and camel hair topcoat. City clothes. This was an Ian she barely recognized, and a formal one which made her feel slightly uncomfortable. Aside from Max, who prided himself on his sartorial elegance, men seldom wore suits in Cobb's Landing. "Are you going somewhere?"

Ian worked for Max as his personal attorney and investment banker. His hobby was running Ian's Booke Nooke, located on Main Street across from Tom's Tools. Ian and Peggy had become somewhat of an item in Cobb's Landing since Ian's arrival a few months earlier. Ian was the first steady date in Peggy's life after the death of her husband Tom, when Nicky was still a baby.

"I have to be on a plane this morning," said Ian. "Business for Max. You know I can't tell you any more than that."

"When will you be back?"

"I'm not sure. My return is open-ended."

"Oh."

Ian wrapped his arms around Peggy and held her close. She inhaled the spicy scent of his now familiar aftershave and knew she would miss him very much.

"Peggy, let me give you some advice about Max. He can be a powerful friend, but an even more powerful enemy. You don't want to cross him."

"Is that what all this is about? Because I won't go along with Max's plans for Thanksgiving?"

"Why is Thanksgiving so important to you?"

"Oh, Ian," said Peggy. "Thanksgiving is a lot of

things. It's tradition, it's part of the time when Lavinia and I were kids and our parents were still alive. It's about family and loved ones and being together for one special day. It's watching the Macy's parade, smelling the turkey roasting in the oven, having a big dinner together, falling asleep over football, having a turkey sandwich before bedtime. It's my favorite holiday, and I really resent Max's turning it into another occasion for making a buck off the tourists."

"Don't fight Max too hard on this, Peggy. He has ways of getting what he wants." Ian cupped Peggy's face in his hands, kissed her tenderly goodbye, then left Tom's Tools at a brisk pace.

A few minutes later, Peggy heard the sound of Max's private helicopter rising from the landing pad near the inn.

"Max has ways of getting what he wants?" Peggy whispered to the empty air. "So do I, Ian. So do I."

CHAPTER 9

"MOM, GUESS WHAT?"

"Nicky, you can talk and set the table at the same time. Get a move on. We've got company coming for dinner in half an hour. Why are you so late getting home from school?"

Nicky was dancing with excitement, his eyes glowing. "That's what I'm trying to tell you. We had auditions after school for the Thanksgiving pageant. I got a lead part."

Peggy dumped a pile of silverware on the table. "Forks on the left, knives on the right. What Thanksgiving pageant?"

"The one Max is having Thanksgiving morning at the inn while the tourists are having breakfast. I'm going to be Miles Standish. Isn't that great? We going to have real costumes and everything."

Peggy stopped making dumplings long enough to

hug her son. "Honey, that's wonderful. Tell me more about this pageant. Who else is in it?"

"Maria is Priscilla, and Charlie is John somebody. I get to ask Maria to . . ." Nicky blushed, ". . . marry me."

"Really? I think you'll find that Miles asked Priscilla to marry John because John was too shy to ask Priscilla himself."

"Mom, are you sure?"

"Pretty sure, honey. You can check it out in your history book."

"That's not fair," said Nicky. "I'm going to ask Max if I can switch parts."

Peggy ruffled Nicky's hair.

"Mom, don't do that. I'm not six years old, you know."

"I know, Nicky." Peggy hugged her son again. "It's just that you're growing up so fast."

"What's that smell on your clothes, Mom? It smells like Ian. Is he coming for dinner?"

"Not tonight, sweetie. Ian had to go out of town on business. You finish setting the table while I run upstairs to change."

Peggy took off her sweater and turtleneck and held them in her arms, inhaling the scent of Ian's aftershave. Two tiny tears began to trickle down her cheeks. "Damn you, Max. First Ian and now Nicky? You really fight dirty."

Was it Peggy's imagination or did she really hear the sound of Max's chuckle echoing in her bedroom?

She put the turtleneck and sweater on her bed, on

top of her pillow, then changed into black leggings and a tunic-length black chenille sweater.

When Peggy got back to the kitchen, Lavinia was tossing a huge salad. "Think this'll be enough, PJ?"

"Looks great. What's for dessert?"

"I stopped at Alsop's for one of their apple-cranberry pies. If anyone wants ice cream with it, I put a quart of vanilla in your freezer. Your chicken and dumplings smell heavenly. I'm starving."

Peggy looked at the half-set table. "Where's Nicky?"

"Over at our house. He wanted to talk to Charlie about the Thanksgiving pageant."

"You heard about that?"

"First thing Charlie told me when I walked in the door, PJ. Charlie's psyched because he gets to marry Maria." Lavinia giggled. "That Max really is a devil."

"You think that's funny, Lovey?"

"Come on, PJ. Where's your sense of humor? Of course it's funny. Everyone in Cobb's Landing—and apparently even Max—knows how Charlie and Nicky feel about Maria. It's a schoolyard crush, PJ. They'll outgrow it. And someday they'll all look back on these days and remember them fondly. The way we remember our childhood crushes on Rob Gibson the summer he lived across the street with his grandparents, before the Murphys bought the Gibson house."

"But what about the Macy's parade? I thought we were all going to watch it together, the way we always do."

"So this year we'll tape it. No big deal. It'll give you and me something to watch later in the afternoon while Chuck snores his way through football."

"Hey, Mom," said Nicky, coming into the kitchen with Charlie. "I just saw Mr. McIntyre pull up in front. He's got a lady with him."

"Go open the door, Nicky. They're here for dinner. That lady is Emily."

"Is she Mr. McIntyre's new girlfriend?"

"Yes, she is, Nicky."

"Cool."

"Go on, Nicky, open the door. Don't keep them standing out there in the cold."

Peggy felt the blast of cold air come through the house and into the kitchen when Nicky opened the front door. Then she saw the flash of black and white cat. Pie hissed at the sight of Holstein and took a flying leap from the floor to the kitchen counter to the top of the refrigerator.

Then, in a slow motion nightmare, Pie took a wrong turn off the refrigerator and landed on the top shelf of a set of standards-and-brackets kitchen wall shelves Peggy had filled with herbs growing in containers of dirt, pots of honey, jars full of brandied fruit, and assorted cookbooks. The shelves collapsed like an old building wired for demolition. The last thing Peggy saw before a badly frightened Pie raced out of the kitchen was the mushroom cloud of dust filling the air.

On the kitchen floor, oozing like repugnant slime from under the fallen cookbooks, shelves, and brackets, was a slowly spreading mass of dirt, herbs, brandied fruit, broken glass, and honey. Peggy didn't know whether to scream or cry. She stood staring at the mess in horror. Then Peggy screamed at the top of her lungs, a primal scream born of anger and frustration. "Damn you, Prunella! I could kill you and that wretched cat!"

Lavinia clamped her own mouth shut. She swallowed hard and grabbed Holstein, pausing long enough to say, "I'll deal with the cat, then we'll take dinner over to my house."

As Lavinia flew out Peggy's front door, holding Holstein stiff-armed in front of her, Emily took one look at the cat and said, "Is that Holstein?" Emily began shaking uncontrollably and clung to Stu for support.

Chuck entered Peggy's kitchen through the back door. "My God," he said. "What happened in here? It looks like Nagasaki after the bomb blast."

All Peggy could do was gesture helplessly. There were no more words left to express her feelings.

"Where's Lavinia?"

"Here, Chuck." On her heels were Stu, Emily, Nicky, and Charlie.

"Hey, man." Chuck and Stu greeted each other with a soft punch on the shoulder. "Good to see you."

"Chuck, this is Emily, Stu's fiancée. Emily, my husband Chuck Cooper. The boys are Nicky, Peggy's son, and my son Charlie. PJ, forget about the mess, I'll help you clean it up later. Let's get dinner moved to my house. Everyone grab something. On the double." Lavinia clapped her hands twice for emphasis, then picked up the kettle of chicken and dumplings.

"Chuck, you take the salad. Nicky, there's a quart of ice cream in the freezer. Charlie, take the pie and don't drop it. Come on, everybody, we'll go through the back."

When the feast had been moved to the Coopers' kitchen, Stu opened the jug of wine he'd brought. Lavinia poured a glass and handed it to Peggy. "Drink up, PJ. This will make you feel better. It's medicinal."

Peggy smiled wanly and began drinking the wine. The glass was quickly emptied and she held it out for a refill. Then she turned to Emily. "I'm really sorry about this. I'd planned such a nice dinner to welcome you to Cobb's Landing."

Lavinia coerced Charlie and Nicky into setting the table. "PJ, why don't you and Emily go into the living room for a few minutes? Stu, Emily needs a glass of wine. I'll call you when dinner's on the table. Chuck, there's a loaf of French bread on the counter. Pop it in the oven, will you?"

In the living room, Peggy said to Emily, "You look a little shaken, are you all right?"

"It was seeing Holstein again. That was Holstein, wasn't it?"

Peggy nodded. "That cat is a menace. He reminds me of that awful cat in *Cinderella*."

Unshed tears glistening in her eyes, Emily leaned toward Peggy. "That cat killed . . ."

Before Emily could complete her sentence, there was a brisk knock on the Cooper's front door. Like the thirteenth fairy at the christening, Prunella Post entered the Cooper's house uninvited and unwelcome.

Emily's face was frozen in a mask of horror, like one of the victims at Pompeii.

Prunella smiled malevolently at her former daughter-in-law. "Hello, Emily. I told you we'd see each other again. You don't think the past is dead and buried, do you?"

Peggy put down her wine glass and rose, her left hand resting lightly on Emily's right shoulder.

Lavinia swooped into the living room like a bird of prey intent on nailing a rodent. "I'll handle this, PJ. She's on *my* turf now." Lavinia advanced toward Prunella until they were face to face, forcing Prunella to retreat in quick small steps. As Prunella backed out of the living room, Lavinia kept moving forward. "You listen to me and listen good, Prunella Post. You are not welcome in my home, and the next time I find you on my property, I'll have you arrested for trespassing."

Prunella's last words were directed at Emily: "I'll make you sorry for what you did to my son. You just wait and see."

CHAPTER 10

PEGGY PICKED AT THE CHICKEN AND DUMPLINGS on her plate. "Fine welcome home party this turned out to be. Emily was so upset she and Stu left before dinner; my kitchen is a disaster area. Can anything else go wrong today?"

"The chicken was real good, Mom." Nicky got up and hugged his mother. "That Mrs. Post is a turkey."

"Yeah," said Charlie. "She sure is. She even looks like one in that dorky brown coat she always wears."

Nicky and Charlie began laughing and making turkey noises. "Gobble, gobble, gobble."

"All right, boys," said Lavinia, a smile tugging at her lips. "That's enough. Haven't you two got homework to do? First clear the table, then we'll have pie and ice cream for dessert."

By ten o'clock the boys were fast asleep, homework done for the next school day, and Peggy's kitchen floor was free of the sticky mess. Chuck promised he'd make a new set of shelves that would bolt to the wall. "Not even an earthquake will take them down, Peggy."

Peggy found a still-trembling Pie hiding under her bed. She coaxed the cat into the open and sat cross-legged on her bedroom carpet, slowly stroking Pie's velvet-black fur. The simple act soothed them both into lethargy. When Pie was calmed to gentle purrs, Peggy lifted the sleepy cat to her bed and placed her on top of the flannel-covered comforter. Peggy changed into her nighttime sweatshirt and pants and eased herself into bed beside the sleeping cat. Peggy drifted off to sleep, inhaling the faint scent of Ian's aftershave still clinging to her pillow.

One by one the lights went out in the little houses arranged in orderly rows on the streets of Cobb's Landing. By midnight, only the streetlights illuminated the swirling snow beginning to accumulate to depths of six to eight inches.

Most residents slumbered peacefully; but in more than one bedroom that night, dark deeds were being plotted.

CHAPTER 11

"NICKY? NICKY! ARE YOU AWAKE?"

"Mom, it's Saturday. Let me sleep."

"Nicky, it's not Saturday. You're still dreaming. Wake up, honey. It's Tuesday and you've got school. It snowed last night. If you want a ride with Chuck and Charlie, you'd better hurry."

Peggy quickly dressed and went to the kitchen to make Nicky a hot breakfast of instant oatmeal. Nicky wasn't crazy about oatmeal, but he'd choke down the apple cinnamon variety if Peggy topped it with brown sugar.

By the time Nicky had finished breakfast and gone to school, and Peggy was headed on foot for Tom's Tools, the pristine snow on the sidewalks was already sullied by footprints.

As Peggy turned onto Main Street, she glanced over at the town square. It looked like a picture postcard with soft mounds of fresh white snow accented by green pines and framed by the snow-splotched bare branches of the trees etched against the brightening sky.

A spot of orange near the middle of the snowscape caught Peggy's eye.

She changed direction and walked to the edge of the village green.

Peggy stared at a brown mound atop the snow. Before her brain could assimilate enough visual data to draw any conclusions, Stu approached from the direction of Max's inn.

"Peggy, have you seen Emily?"

"What?"

"Emily? I can't find her."

"When did you see her last?"

Stu hesitated before saying, "I'm not sure."

"What do you mean, you're not sure?"

"When I woke up this morning, she was gone. The car is still in the inn parking lot."

"Elementary, my dear Watson. Emily must be on foot."

"Duh, Peggy. Even I figured out that much."

"Stu, she probably went for a walk. Emily will turn up soon. Trust me. You know there aren't that many places to go in Cobb's Landing." Peggy pointed to the orange knit hat and brown down coat. "I think right now we have more serious problems than your missing fiancée. Unless I'm mistaken, that's Prunella Post lying face down in the snow. As of this minute, you're back on duty as our police chief."

"Is she dead?" asked Stu.

"I don't know. She doesn't appear to be moving."

"Did you touch anything?"

"Of course not," Peggy snapped. "I know better. Besides, I just got here myself."

"What's that sticking out of her coat?" asked Stu.

They both leaned forward to get a better look. A silvery stiletto-like object with a looped handle protruded from the middle of Prunella Post's back. They stepped back in horror when they realized they were looking at a possible murder scene.

"Peggy, go call an ambulance while I guard the area."

Peggy ran to Tom's Tools, but stopped abruptly when she saw her shattered store window. Petty vandalism was unheard of in Cobb's Landing before it became Colonial Village and began attracting strangers to the little town on a daily basis. Peggy's carefully arranged mobile display of Thanksgiving cooking utensils was now a haphazard heap of fallen objects.

Peggy muttered a stream of four letter words that, had they come out of her son's mouth, would have resulted in Nicky's being grounded for the rest of his life after his mouth had been thoroughly washed with strong soap. Peggy went into the hardware store, called the hospital for an ambulance, then ran back to the village green where Stu stood watch.

"My store's been broken into," said Peggy.

"When?"

"How do I know? Everything was fine when I locked up last night at five."

"Is anything missing?"

Peggy threw up her hands in total frustration. "Stu, get a grip. I don't know. My store window is broken, my Thanksgiving display destroyed. I went inside long enough to call the hospital for an ambulance." Before Stu could ask any more questions, Peggy said, "No, I didn't touch anything other than the front door and the inside phone. I want you to investigate."

"Calm down, Peggy. I'll get to it. Which job do you want me to tackle first? This one?" Stu pointed to Prunella Post. "Your broken store window? Or my missing fiancée?"

Peggy rolled her eyes. For a Tuesday, the day was shaping up into another lousy Monday.

Stu pointed to small tracks in the snow around Prunella. "Looks like an animal has been here. If I'm not mistaken, those are paw prints."

"Holstein?" asked Peggy. She looked around. "Where is that wretched cat?" Peggy heard faint yowls but couldn't place the origin of the sound. "Stu, do you see the cat? I keep hearing him, but I can't see him."

Peggy and Stu swept the snowscape with their eyes and saw nothing. Finally Peggy looked at the trees bordering the green. On a middle branch of a giant oak sat Holstein, his black and white fur blending with the snow mounded on the bark. Peggy tugged at Stu's sleeve and pointed. "There he is."

"Oh, geez," said Stu, "that's all I need. A cat in a tree. How are we going to get him down?"

"What do you want to do? Question him? Leave him be. When he gets hungry, he'll come down."

The ambulance, siren blaring, approached on Main Street, trailed by Dale Hansen, the new county medical examiner, in his own car.

"I heard your call, Peggy, and thought I'd tag along in case I was needed," said Dale. He knelt in the snow beside Prunella Post for his examination, then looked up at Peggy. "I'm sorry. This woman is dead. Was she a friend of yours?"

"Her name is Prunella Post, but I hardly knew her," said Peggy. "She arrived in Cobb's Landing only three days ago. She was planning on spending the winter here."

"What is this imbedded in her back?" asked Dale. "It looks like something out of someone's kitchen. I think my wife has one of these." He began taking a series of photographs of the body where it lay in the snow.

Peggy looked closer at the metal object. Her heart sank when she recognized what it was. "Ummmm, I know what that is," she said. "It's a turkey skewer. I had them on display in my store window. But the window was broken sometime during the night, so that skewer might have come from my store. Do you think it killed her?"

"I won't know the cause of death until I've completed my examination," said Dale. "Who's in charge of police matters in Cobb's Landing these days?"

"I am," said Stu.

"Back on the job again, eh?"

Stu nodded.

"Does anyone have anything else to add before we move the body?"

"Mrs. Post said she had a heart condition," said Peggy. "She carried a small pewter pillbox with her at all times. It was usually in her pocket."

"Thanks, Peggy," said Dale. "That's good to know." He felt inside the slash pockets of Prunella Post's down coat. "There's no pillbox there now."

"Call me when your report is ready," Stu said to the medical examiner. To Peggy he added, "I'm going to look for Emily."

"Don't forget my store window," said Peggy. "I need to get it replaced as soon as possible."

"I'll meet you at the hardware store," said Stu. "Give me fifteen minutes."

Peggy watched as Prunella Post's body was lifted from the snow and moved to the ambulance.

From his vantage point in the tree, Holstein also watched the proceedings. When the body of his mistress was no longer visible, he lowered his head onto his front paws and meowed plaintively.

As the ambulance headed slowly up Main Street, on the far side of the square a figure in a green hooded coat slipped away from the protective coloration of the pines.

CHAPTER 12

"I'M YOUR BEST FRIEND, PJ," SAID LAVINIA. "I can't believe you didn't call me when you found Prunella in the snow. I'm a trained medical professional. I could have told you right away the woman was dead."

"Lovey, there was so much going on at once I didn't have time to think. First Prunella, then Stu going on about Emily being missing, then my broken store window. Bad things really do come in threes."

"Let's go over to Clemmie's for coffee and a muffin," said Lavinia. "Your treat. I'd help you clean up the mess, but I've got to get to the hospital for my noon-to-eight shift. At least this time there's no oozing sticky stuff to clean."

They walked across snow-covered Main Street to Clemmie's Cafe.

"Hey Peggy," called out a voice from the back of

Clemmie's, "are we ever gonna get our streets plowed?"

"When the snow is over twelve inches, we plow. If we plowed for every flake of snow, the town would be even more in the red than it is now."

When the coffee and hot cran-apple muffins were on the table, Peggy raised her cup. "To Prunella Post." Peggy sipped her coffee, then put the cup on the table. "I wish I felt sorrier about her death."

"To Prunella." Lavinia sipped her own coffee. "What will become of Holstein?"

"Oh, shoot. I knew I forgot something. I've got to call Claudia Lewis." Peggy went to the wall phone next to the cash register and punched in Claudia's number. "Claudia, it's Peggy. . . . You heard already? . . . Yes, it's true about Prunella Post. But it's Holstein I'm concerned about. He's up a tree on the town square. Could you come and help me get him down? I'm at Clemmie's having coffee with Lavinia. I'll wait for you here."

"Thanks for reminding me, Lovey," Peggy said as she got back to the table. "I forgot all about Holstein. He's up a tree on the green. Claudia's coming to help me get him down."

"You hate that cat, PJ."

"I know." Peggy sighed. "But my conscience won't let me leave him there to starve in the cold. It's not his fault Prunella was so impossible. Maybe Claudia can find a good home for him."

It took three cans of tuna to lure Holstein down from the tree. Claudia wrapped her arms around the cat and gazed into his amber eyes. To Peggy's surprise,

Holstein began to purr and reached out to tap Claudia's cheek with his paw. Claudia rubbed her nose against Holstein's face. "He really is a sweet cat, Peggy. I'll be glad to take care of him until someone claims him."

"He likes to watch the Weather Channel," said Peggy. "With the sound muted."

Claudia laughed. "Holstein and I will get along just fine. I like the Weather Channel, too. Especially now when it's freezing cold here and so warm in Hawaii. Every winter I dream about swimming in those azure waters." Claudia slipped Holstein into a carrier and put him in the back of her four-wheel-drive SUV.

"Be careful, Claudia. That's when he peed all over my back seat."

"I keep mine covered with an old plastic shower curtain." Claudia waved and headed back to her animal clinic.

When Peggy finally got back to Tom's Tools, Stu was waiting outside.

"Holstein is now at Claudia Lewis's clinic," said Peggy. "Did you find Emily?"

"She was having breakfast in the dining room when I got back to the inn," replied Stu. "You were right, Peggy. Emily couldn't sleep and went for a walk."

"Did you tell her about Prunella?"

Stu nodded. "I hated being the messenger, but Emily took it well." Stu reached in his pocket for a notebook. "Give me all the details on the break-in here at the store."

"Not much to tell Stu. When I came to use the phone I found my store window broken."

"Anything missing?"

"From the window? It's hard to tell, everything I had on display is now heaped in the bottom of the display area."

"What about the store? You see anything missing?"

"Stu, give me a break. How would I know? This is a hardware store. I sell screws, nuts, bolts. I don't have time to take inventory to see if any are missing."

"Money?"

"You know I don't keep any money in the store overnight. I drop my deposit at the bank on the way home, and the change for the next day . . . never mind where I keep that."

"I've already taken pictures outside; I'll take a few inside." Stu pulled a disposable camera from his pocket and snapped a few pictures. "It's a waste of time to dust for prints. I'll give you a report and copies of the pictures for your insurance company."

Peggy sighed. In order to keep the store insurance premiums down, the deductible was so high that the cost of replacing the window would come out of her own pocket.

"You know, we never did have dinner last night. How about if you and Emily come over tonight and we'll pretend last night never happened."

"Thanks, Peggy. Emily would like that."

"Same time, same place." Peggy impulsively hugged Stu. "I know this isn't the welcome home you were expecting, but I'm glad you're back. We'll do our best to make Emily feel at home in Cobb's Landing." Peggy handed Stu a set of keys. "I think you'll find your office pretty much the way you left it."

Peggy called the glass company to replace her window, then picked up the broom and began sweeping glass. When she started recreating her Thanksgiving window display, her worst fear came true.

A turkey skewer was missing from the kitchen implements she'd hung in the store window.

CHAPTER 13

THE MEAT LOAF AND BAKED POTATOES PEGGY had rustled together for dinner for Emily and Stu had disappeared into crumbs on plates. Throughout dinner, conversation had revolved around stories about Cobb's Landing and the history of the town before Max appeared on the scene—Prunella Post was never mentioned once—but as Peggy was cutting into a pie from Alsop's Bakery, Stu cleared his throat.

"Out with it, Peggy Jean. I've known you all your life, and I know when you're keeping something from me."

Peggy served coffee and dessert—pumpkin pie topped with cinnamon ice cream—before she spoke.

"There was something missing from my store window. A turkey skewer." Peggy picked up a brown paper bag from the kitchen counter and handed it to

Stu. "Here's another one from the same set. You can take it to Dale Hansen to see if it's a match."

"Match to what?" asked Emily.

Peggy glanced at Stu. "Didn't you tell her?"

"Tell me what?" asked Emily.

Stu cleared his throat a second time, sounding like a cat trying to eject a furball.

"I'll tell her," said Peggy. There were times when Stu was such a spineless wimp that Peggy wanted to thump him on the head. "There was a turkey skewer protruding from the back of Prunella's coat when she was found face down in the snow this morning."

"Someone stabbed Prunella to death?" asked Emily, adding "serves her right" under her breath.

Peggy turned to look at Emily. Had Emily really said "serves her right"? Peggy replied gently, "We won't know for sure until Dale Hansen submits his report. She may have died of natural causes. I understand Prunella had a heart condition."

Emily nodded. "It's true. At least that's what she always said."

"She carried around a box of pills with her," said Peggy.

Emily nodded again. "A little round pewter pillbox. It's an antique. Alan, her son, gave it to her for her birthday. It's engraved inside the lid with the initials PP."

"We didn't find it this morning," said Stu. "I went back and looked everywhere in the snow for it."

Chuck came in the back door. "Hey, Stu. Saw your car out front. Lavinia's stuck at the hospital for another couple of hours. How about coming over to my house for a brew? Peggy and Emily can talk about girl stuff for a while."

Peggy snorted and stuck out her tongue at Chuck. He'd pay for that "girl stuff" remark. Emily nodded at Stu. Stu and Chuck headed out the back, through the fence gate, and into the Cooper's kitchen.

"More coffee, Emily?" Peggy said brightly.

"You wouldn't happen to have something a little stronger than coffee?"

Peggy went to the cupboard and pulled out a half-full bottle of brandy. "Will this do? I'm not much of a drinker."

"That will be great, thank you."

Peggy poured two small glasses of brandy, refilled her coffee cup, and sat down at the table.

Emily took one small sip of brandy, then burst into tears.

Peggy didn't know quite what to do. Had it been Lavinia crying at her kitchen table, Peggy would have gotten out a box of tissue, then hugged her friend. But Emily was a total stranger. Peggy reached for the tissue box and set it in front of Emily. She patted Emily's shoulder, then sat down to drink coffee.

When Emily's tears had subsided, she pulled a handful of tissues from the box, then took another sip of brandy. "You must think I'm an awful ninny, sitting here crying in your kitchen when I don't even know you. But I feel like I've been holding my breath ever since Stu told me Prunella was dead. I've just got to talk to someone."

"Help yourself to the brandy." Peggy put the bottle on the table, then sat with her chin resting on her hands looking at Emily. "I'm a good listener. Tell me about Prunella's son. You said his name is Alan?"

As Emily began to talk, Peggy wasn't sure if Emily was directing the conversation to her or merely talking aloud, but she sat quietly and listened.

"Alan and I met our senior year at Ohio State. We got married after graduation. We eloped. Alan said it would be more romantic to get married that way. I found out later it was because he didn't want to tell his mother about me."

Oh God, thought Peggy.

"We moved to a small town in Ohio. I got a job teaching. I teach elementary school. Alan passed his CPA exam and was setting up his own business as an accountant. A few months later there was a knock at the door and there stood Prunella. She'd hired a private detective to track down her son." Emily drained the brandy glass and refilled it. "In a matter of weeks she'd moved to the same town—she rented a house across the street from us—bringing Holstein with her. See, Prunella was a widow and Alan was her only child."

Peggy nodded sympathetically and thought, I've heard this story before. It's what Agatha Christie's Jane Marple would call a village parallel.

"I got pregnant and we had a baby boy. Prunella practically lived at our house. Alan and I hardly had a minute to ourselves. Prunella was always underfoot or calling Alan to come over and do something for her, like changing a light bulb or carrying in her groceries or taking care of her yard. She used her heart problem as an excuse. One night Alan and I made plans to go out, just the two of us. Nothing fancy, a bite to eat and a movie. Prunella insisted on babysitting. We got home to find an ambulance at our front door. Our son was dead. It was ruled as Sudden Infant Death Syndrome."

Peggy reached over to squeeze Emily's hand. Without missing a beat, Emily continued her softspoken monologue. "I never believed it. I know Holstein smothered my son. I found cat hair all over his crib. I had a nervous breakdown and spent the next few weeks in a private hospital. When I was released, I found out that Alan had already started divorce proceedings. Prunella convinced Alan that it was my fault our son had died, that if I hadn't insisted we go out that night, just the two of us, our son would still be alive."

"Prunella was a monster," said Peggy, pouring more coffee.

Emily refilled her brandy glass. "I thought my life was over. I moved into a women's shelter until I got my bearings. Then I packed my clothes and moved, starting over again, teaching sixth grade in a small town."

"What became of Alan?"

"He died a few months later in a car accident. The police said he was drunk at the time. Prunella vowed she would never forgive me for ruining her son's life. She said his death would always be on my head."

"Prunella Post was certifiably insane," said Peggy. "And a giant pain, in the bargain."

Emily nodded in agreement, then stared at the tabletop. "There's one thing that frightens me."

"What's that?" asked Peggy.

"It's no secret that I hated Prunella," said Emily. "Please don't tell Stu what I've told you. He knows I was married to Alan, but he doesn't know all the details. I'll tell Stu myself when the time is right. If he finds out now, I'm afraid he'll think I killed Prunella."

"That's absurd," said Peggy. "Stu would never think such a thing. He loves you. He's planning to marry you."

"If Stu doesn't suspect me, then who will he suspect? You?" Emily looked directly at Peggy, a laser-like stare that made Peggy feel like a goose was walking on her grave. Emily poured the last drops of brandy into her glass as she said, "Tonight you admitted that the murder weapon—what was it? a turkey skewer?—had come from your hardware store. You're as likely a suspect as I am. Or would be, unless you keep your mouth shut."

Peggy took Emily's brandy glass and drained it in one swallow.

CHAPTER 14

WHEN STU AND EMILY HAD GONE BACK TO Max's inn, Lavinia sat in Emily's chair nursing a cup of coffee.

"My God, poor Emily," said Lavinia. "Do you believe everything she said?"

"What reason would I have to doubt her?" asked Peggy.

"You've got to admit, PJ, this is the plot of a soap opera. Elopement, crazy possessive mother, dead baby, stint in a mental hospital, son dies in a car crash, mother vows revenge. Mother stalks former daughter-in-law, then found stabbed to death in the snow." Lavinia giggled as she mimed playing a tiny violin with her fingertips. "It's better than the movie *Soapdish*."

"Or endless *Law & Order* reruns," added Peggy. "Emily asked me not to tell Stu."

"Did you?"

"What?"

"Promise?"

"I didn't say anything. Not yes or no. She didn't use the word 'promise.' She said 'please don't tell Stu.' There's a big difference, Lovey."

"Hair-splitting difference, PJ. She's asking you to keep your mouth shut. That's not something you ask a stranger. No matter how well we know Stu, Emily is still a stranger."

"She also said something that made me feel really creepy."

"What?"

"Emily said that it was no secret that she hated Prunella and if Stu knew all the details about her past she would be the major suspect in Prunella's death. But, if I kept my mouth shut about what she'd said, then Stu would suspect me because the turkey skewer in Prunella's back came from my hardware store."

"Oh, geez." Lavinia let out a low whistle. "Emily is one slick manipulator. She's got you between a rock and a hard place, PJ. If you rat her out to Stu, it'll sound like you did it to save your own hide."

Peggy nodded. "I know. Either way, I'm screwed."

Once again, Peggy thought she heard the sound of Max's sardonic chuckle. It had to be only her imagination. Or was it?

"What's that look, PJ? You look like you've seen a ghost."

"No ghost, Lovey. But I keep hearing Max laughing up his sleeve."

"Max? What's he got to do with anything?"

"That's what I'd like to know, Lovey."

"Forget Max. He's a legend in his own mind. Tell me one thing, PJ."

"What?"

"Did you kill Prunella Post?"

Peggy stared at her best friend. "Are you nuts? Of course I didn't kill her."

Lavinia hugged Peggy, then headed for the back door. "That's all I needed to know, PJ. Your word is good enough for me. We'll solve the mystery of Prunella Post's death before the snow is deep enough to plow."

Lavinia's words may have sounded prophetic, but they proved highly inaccurate. By the next morning, the snow was over a foot deep and more was on the way.

Peggy woke to a freezing cold house. She could actually see her breath hanging in cloud-like puffs in the frosty air. She ran down to the basement to check the furnace. She had plenty of fuel, but the furnace was stone cold dead. Damn. She ran back to the kitchen to call Slim, the handyman who specialized in furnace repair. In her next life not only would she own a hardware store, but she'd also be an auto mechanic, electrician, plumber, and able to fix anything in thirty seconds with a Q-tip and piece of wire like MacGyver.

Her next call was to the Cobb's Landing plowing crew, headed by Bob, who ran the local gas station. Peggy didn't want to think how much plowing the streets would cost the town. She definitely didn't want to think about how much fixing her furnace was going to cost her personally.

Peggy sighed and went upstairs to wake Nicky. "Honey, time to get up for school. Get dressed before breakfast, the furnace is out and it's cold in here." Peggy went back to the kitchen to turn on the electric oven for warmth and to make Nicky a hot breakfast. He'd complain about having oatmeal again, but it was the best she could do when she was shivering so hard she could barely hold a coffee cup steady in her trembling hands.

Nicky appeared in the kitchen with his hands tucked into the sleeves of his sweatshirt. "Why is it so cold in here, Mom?"

"I told you honey, the furnace went out. Slim is on his way over to check it out. I made you some hot cocoa, with lots of mini-marshmallows. That should help warm you. Eat your oatmeal while it's hot."

Peggy heard the sound of a snow plow coming up her street. It stopped in front of her house and Slim jumped out and ran up to her door.

"I've got a minute to look at your furnace, Peggy," said Slim. He was bundled from head to toe in a heavy jacket, hat, scarf, and thick boots. He stomped his feet on Peggy's sisal welcome mat before entering the house. "If I can't get it going now, I'll come back after I've finished plowing." Slim disappeared into Peggy's basement and came back a few minutes later, shaking his head. "This will take some time to fix, Peggy. How old is that furnace?"

Peggy thought for a minute. "I don't know. It's been in the house as long as I can remember."

"Peggy, you grew up in this house. That furnace is probably older than you are. It's time to think about buying a new one."

Peggy sighed. All she could see were dollar signs dancing before her eyes. She batted them away like a swarm of pesky summer gnats.

Slim patted Peggy's shoulder. "I'll get it running somehow. Don't you worry. Leave a key under the mat, I'll get back here when I can." Slim stopped halfway back to the plow and turned to Peggy. "Bob says can you order more salt and sand? Long hard winter coming, according to the rings on the woolly bears, and we don't want to get caught short."

The plowed snow was blocking Peggy's car in her garage. She decided to walk to Tom's Tools but knew she couldn't leave Pie and Buster to fend for themselves in the shivering cold house. She wrapped Pie in an old towel and put her into her cat carrier, clipped a leash to Buster's collar, and set off trudging through the snow, fresh flakes falling on her head as she walked.

Tom's Tools was toasty warm. By the time she'd released Pie from her carrier and rubbed dry a snowy wet Buster, Peggy was sweating in her turtleneck and thick sweater. If she had to choose between too cold and too warm, Peggy would take too warm every time. If Slim couldn't get her furnace going, she and Nicky could stay in front of the fireplace at home, or at the hardware store. Or in a pinch at the Murphys' house. The Murphys! Had anyone called Gerald and Sara to tell them they no longer had a tenant for the winter?

After Peggy ordered more salt and sand for the town's winter storm supplies, she placed a call to Sara Murphy.

"No, Sara, Prunella Post didn't die in your house. . . . Yes, I realize this is an unfortunate turn of events. If you'll get in touch with your leasing agent, I'll make sure that all of Prunella's things are removed from your house. . . . The cat? He's with Claudia Lewis. By the way, my furnace is acting up. If Slim can't get it fixed, is it all right if Nicky and I stay at your house for a night or two? . . . Thank you, Sara. . . . Yes, I'll keep in touch. Love to you and Gerald."

"My, my, my. Looks like we've got trouble in River City. And it begins with a P which rhymes with T." Max stood rubbing his hands, one might almost say gleefully. On a cold, snowy day, Max was dressed in his suit, spotless shirt, and red silk bow tie without even a drop of melted snow marring his impeccable appearance.

Peggy glanced outside. The snow had diminished to blowing flurries. The few people walking about on Main Street or shoveling their storefront walks were bundled to their chins, hoods pulled over their heads to keep the snow out of their faces. Max looked like he'd just stepped out of his tailor's on a bright spring day.

"Max, how do you do it?"

"Do what?" Max adopted his pose of complete innocence, perfected over years of practice.

"Never mind," Peggy said crossly, knowing she'd never get a straight answer from Max no matter how many times she tried. "What can I do for you today?"

"Are you ready to talk turkey?"

"Is that what all this is about?" Peggy glared at Max as if he'd taken leave of his senses. "You want to talk about Thanksgiving when I'm knee deep in a body on the green, a broken store window, and a dead furnace?"

"Had enough, Mayor?" Max said softly.

"Max, get to the point. I'm very busy. I have a business to run." Peggy opened her inventory ledger and began making entries.

Max looked at Peggy for a long silent moment.

When Peggy looked up from her ledger, Max was gone. Only the echo of his chuckle hung in the air as a reminder of his presence.

•

CHAPTER 15

WHEN PEGGY FINISHED HER INVENTORY, SHE realized she'd sold almost two dozen sets of turkey skewers in the past few days in addition to roasting pans, basters, meat thermometers, and wooden spoons. Most of the sales had been to Cobb's Landing residents, but a few were to tourists. How would she ever track down the skewer imbedded in Prunella Post's back? The skewers were mass-produced, not numbered limited editions. It would be as daunting a task as finding that proverbial needle in a haystack.

As much as Peggy detested Prunella Post, she knew she hadn't killed her, but had no way of proving her innocence.

"Damn!" Peggy yowled in frustration.

"Have I come at a bad time, Peggy?" Peggy looked up at Slim. "I've got good news and bad news. Which do you want first?"

"Oh, give me the bad news and get it over with. Then I'll have something good to look forward to."

"I got your furnace going," said Slim.

"That's the bad news?"

"No, that's the good news. The bad news is you need parts, and the ones you need have been discontinued. They don't make them anymore, Peggy."

"What are you saying, Slim?"

"You really need a new furnace, Peggy. I can cobble together a few parts in Bob's welding shop, but you'll be lucky to get through the winter."

"Anything you can do to keep the old one going will be much appreciated, Slim. Bring me your bill and I'll pay you in cash."

Slim winked and nodded. Like many residents in Cobb's Landing, he often worked under the table for undeclared cash.

When Slim was gone, Peggy got her bankbooks out of her purse. She was very careful to keep her business and personal finances completely separate. She looked at the balance in her personal checking account. There was enough to cover groceries and her monthly bills, but not enough to cover a new furnace. The only account with that much money was Nicky's college fund. Peggy made a solemn vow the day she opened the account that no matter what happened she would never touch it for any reason except Nicky's education.

The only other options were a bank loan or putting the new furnace on her credit card, but Peggy hated debt more than lima beans. Boy, did she hate lima beans. Even the thought of those dry pasty green things made her throat close. Peggy crossed her fingers that Slim could pull off a minor miracle and vowed to start saving for a new furnace. Her dream of buying a new car would just have to wait awhile longer.

Stu ambled into Tom's Tools about noon. "How about this snow, Peggy? Must be a record for so early in the year."

Something Max had said recently tickled at the back of Peggy's brain, but she couldn't quite grasp it.

"Any news from Dale Hansen?" asked Peggy.

"Not yet, but it's only been a day. I would have dropped off the turkey skewer you gave me, but the roads are impassable on account of the snow."

"I talked to Sara Murphy this morning. I offered to pack up Prunella's things so the house can be rented again. I'd like you to help me. We can make an inventory for Prunella's next of kin."

"I'm not sure there is any next of kin, Peggy."

"How do you know? She must have somebody, somewhere."

"Emily hinted that Prunella didn't have any family left."

"Really? You talked to Emily about Prunella?"

"I tried, but she didn't want to discuss it."

Peggy gestured to Stu to help himself to coffee, then she settled herself on the high-backed stool behind the checkout counter. "Tell me, Stu. How did you and Emily meet?"

Stu mumbled into his coffee cup.

"I didn't catch that. What did you say?"

"Online dating service."

Peggy's jaw was about to drop, but she recovered in time. "Really? I've wondered about those. Tell me all about it."

Stu gave Peggy a crash course into the world of online dating. After completing a lengthy questionnaire, he'd been matched with several women and had chosen Emily. They corresponded by email for a few weeks and finally arranged to meet. It was love at first sight. Within two weeks they were engaged and making plans to come to Cobb's Landing.

"Just like that?"

"Just like that." Stu smiled. "I know Emily's the one."

"Stu," Peggy said gently, "I hope you're right. You deserve to be happy."

"You do too, Peggy. How's it going with Ian? You two still an item? You were when I left."

Peggy waggled her hand in the air. "Ian and I are still getting to know each other. But let's talk about you. Tell me more about Emily. Just how well do you know her? You seemed surprised to find out she'd been married before."

"Emily explained all that. It wasn't a happy marriage. Having met her mother-in-law I can understand why she didn't want to talk about it. I know I can make Emily happy."

"I'm sure you can, Stu. Has Emily met your mother yet?"

Again Stu mumbled into his coffee cup.

"What did you say?"

"Not yet. I've been, ah, busy with police business."

"Right. Have you talked to your mother since you got back?"

"I'm going over there this afternoon to shovel her sidewalk."

"Ah."

"What does that mean?"

"Nothing. Nothing at all. What about children? Does Emily have any children?"

"What is this interest in Emily?"

"Stu, we grew up together. I've known you all your life and I want you to be happy. Just don't rush quite so fast, okay? Have you told Emily about your marital past?"

"Don't nag. You sound like my mother."

"I'm not nagging. I'm giving advice. That's not nagging." Peggy smiled. "You promised me you would talk to Emily. She's going to find out sooner or later, Stu. Cobb's Landing is still a very small town and people will assume she knows. It's not ancient history, you know. It's still pretty fresh in people's minds. Better Emily should hear it from you."

"I have to go, Peggy. My mother is expecting me." Stu put his empty coffee cup on the counter and headed for the door. "By the way, don't leave town without letting me know."

"What?"

"I'm investigating a suspicious death, Peggy. Right now you're my only suspect. We all heard you threaten to kill Prunella Post."

Before Peggy could defend herself, Stu left Tom's Tools without saying another word.

CHAPTER 16

PEGGY AND LAVINIA WERE SITTING IN TOM'S Tools drinking coffee, watching sky-sifted snow waft to the ground in a fine powder.

"Stu McIntyre is blowing smoke, PJ. He's grabbing at straws and you know it. Don't let him rattle you. Did you tell him about Emily?"

"Oh, Lovey, I tried. I hinted so broadly that only a fool would miss the point."

"When it comes to romance, Stu McIntyre is an abject fool. We all know that. His past experiences in that department speak for themselves. But let's not dig that up again."

"I did find out something. How Stu and Emily met."

"Do tell. I'm dying to know."

"Through an online dating service."

Lavinia began to laugh. "You've got to be kidding. You mean like that guy on television with the smarmy voice pimping his Internet dating service?"

"I guess so, Lovey. Stu didn't say which one. Just that he met Emily through the service, they emailed for a few weeks, then met in person and made plans to get married."

"Oh, this is rich. Wait until I tell Chuck. It can't be any worse than Stu's other choices. Has Emily met old Mrs. McIntyre?"

"Not yet, from what Stu said. He's been busy with police business."

Lavinia snorted. "Yeah, right. He's still afraid of his mother, just like he was when we were kids."

"Be fair, Lovey. If she were your mother, you'd be afraid of her, too. She scares the devil out of me."

"Doesn't she remind you of someone?"

"Who?"

"Prunella Post." Lavinia sat looking like a cat who has just devoured a large saucer of cream. "If I liked Emily—which I don't because I think she's a slick little manipulator after that crap she pulled on you— I'd warn her to run while she can. She's going from the frying pan to the fire in the mother-in-law department."

"That's her problem, Lovey. Speaking of Prunella, I need you to do me a favor."

"What?"

"I told Sara Murphy I'd go over to their house and pack up Prunella's belongings. I asked Stu to help me, but he never committed himself."

"Sure, I'll help. Let's do it tonight. Charlie and Nicky have rehearsal for the Thanksgiving pageant and Chuck is driving them. Max asked Chuck to help with the scenery."

"When did Max talk to Chuck?"

"This afternoon. Max stopped at the high school. He's got all the kids involved in the pageant. They think it's neat and they're all excited about playing pilgrims and Indians. Max hinted to Chuck that I could help with costumes, but Chuck made it clear that I don't sew."

Peggy laughed. "You're the only one I know who glued her Girl Scout badges to her sash."

Lavinia giggled. "I would have stapled them, but the material was too thick."

Buster roused himself from a nap at the back of the store and walked over to Peggy to be patted.

"What's Buster doing here?"

"My furnace went out last night. The house was freezing cold this morning."

"Why didn't you call me? I would have brought over a couple of space heaters."

"I called Slim. He got it going and thinks he can make some parts for it to get me though the winter. But he says I need a new furnace."

"It's always something with these old houses, isn't it?" said Lavinia. "Chuck says we're going to need new pipes in a year or two. I don't know where we're going to get the money to pay for it. I hate to borrow."

Peggy nodded. "I have to start saving for a new furnace, but damned if I know where to cut my budget. We need to come up with a money-making idea."

"Like stuffing envelopes in our spare time?" Lavinia hooted with laughter.

"That's a scam," said Peggy, looking out the window at the snow piling up on the sidewalk. "Let's go home before the snow gets too deep."

Peggy was loading Pie into her carrier when the phone rang. "Lovey, get that, will you?"

Lavinia answered. "Tom's Tools." Pause. "Gerald? This is Lavinia Cooper. Do you want to talk to Peggy? She's right here. . . . Oh, okay. I'll be glad to give her a message. . . . I know she talked to Sara earlier today. We're going over to your house tonight." As Lavinia listened, a slow smile spread across her face. "That's terrible. Yes, of course. Peggy and I can do it. . . . Yes, that seems very fair. Don't worry about a thing. We're on the job. We'll be in touch. Thank you, Gerald. Love to Sara."

"What was all that about?" asked Peggy as she clipped the leash to Buster's collar.

"PJ, we're in business!" crowed Lavinia.

"Doing what?"

"Gerald Murphy wants us to manage his house. Handle the rental, screen tenants, collect the rent; and here's the best part: he's going to pay us a monthly fee!"

"Really?"

"Even better, he's talking to some other property owners about having us do the same thing for them. Not everyone wants to rent their houses, but we'll keep an eye on the houses when the owners are gone. And get paid for it. How does that sound to you?"

"Like the answer to a prayer," said Peggy. "I wonder what brought this on?"

"I'll tell you," said Lavinia. "Gerald fired the national rental agency he'd hired. He's so mad at them he's spitting tacks."

"Why?"

"Prunella Post's rent check bounced!"

Peggy and Lavinia giggled over Prunella Post's final folly all the way home.

CHAPTER 17

"WILL YOU LOOK AT THIS MESS, PJ? THE WOMAN was a pig!"

Peggy and Lavinia stood in the Murphys' living room, surveying the chaos Prunella had created during her brief tenancy.

"What's that smell?" Lavinia said.

Peggy sniffed the air. "Litter box." Peggy reluctantly followed her nose to the source—a plastic dishpan sitting on newspaper close to the Murphys' back door off the kitchen. Tearing a bag from the roll of heavy-duty trash bags she'd brought from the hardware store, Peggy bagged the litter box and hauled it to the front door and put it outside on the Murphys' front porch.

After clearing the mess of empty soda cans, used coffee cups, and paper plates from the living room, Peggy and Lavinia quickly vacuumed and dusted.

"That's how Sara left it," said Lavinia, surveying the now tidy room, smelling faintly of Lemon Pledge. "We'll have to get an inventory from Sara before we rent the house to anyone else. I'd hate to be responsible if any of Sara's things were broken or missing. Do you think we're really cut out to be rental agents, PJ?"

"Of course we are, Lovey. We can do this. When Ian gets back I'll ask him to draw up the papers we need to cover our butts with owners and tenants."

"Where is Ian? I haven't seen him in days."

"Max sent him off on a business trip."

"Oh really?"

"I think it's one of Max's little ploys to get me to fall in line with his Thanksgiving plans. But I don't cave in that easily."

"You know, PJ . . ." Lavinia hesitated.

Peggy looked at her friend. "Don't tell me Max has gotten to you, too?"

"Not exactly. But he's got everyone in town really excited about the holiday. The kids are busy rehearsing for the pageant, their parents are building scenery and making costumes, Gina and Lew Alsop are at the bakery every night making pies, rolls, and cookies for the feast. Max has even hired the crew at Clemmie's to cook the turkeys and prepare the trimmings. It's going to be a lot of fun, PJ."

"But what about our dinner and our plans? We've already shopped. I thought Chuck wanted to cook his deep-fried turkey."

"Would it be so terrible if we celebrated Thanksgiving on a different day this year?"

"But it won't be Thanksgiving," said Peggy. "It'll just be a turkey dinner. It won't be the same. After all the years we've spent Thanksgiving together, I can't believe you're finking out on me."

"PJ, I didn't say I was bailing out on you. You know I love our holidays together. We're family. You, Nicky, me, Chuck, and Charlie. I just thought this year we might try something different on Thanksgiving. We'll all be together like we always are. Think about it. We could still have dinner together. What if we ate dinner after Thanksgiving football instead of mid-afternoon?"

Peggy sighed. "Let's get the rest of Prunella's stuff packed up. It's getting late and Nicky will be home soon."

They moved to the kitchen and bagged the empty pizza boxes, cat food cans, and take-out cartons from Clemmie's Cafe.

"Prunella didn't spend much time cooking, did she?" commented Peggy, opening the refrigerator. Inside were two cans of soda and an open box of baking soda Sara had left to keep the refrigerator fresh. Peggy handed one can to Lavinia and popped the top on the other for herself. The two women downed the soda as they wiped the kitchen counters and mopped the floor clean of Prunella and Holstein's footprints.

They moved upstairs. On either side of the stairs were bedrooms. One was Gerald and Sara's master bedroom; the other had been converted into a cozy sitting room and study with a pull-out queen-size couch for guests.

Peggy and Lavinia went to the paned windows in

the sitting room. Looking out across the snow-covered street illuminated by the glow of the street lights, they could see their own homes and the windows of their childhood bedrooms.

"This is where Rob Gibson stayed that summer, Lovey."

"Remember how many times we looked out our own windows at this one?"

Peggy and Lavinia smiled at the memories of that long ago time when they were twelve and had mad crushes on the cute teenaged boy spending the summer with his grandparents.

Moving into the master bedroom, they found Prunella's rollabout suitcase and meager assortment of clothes.

"I'll say this much, she traveled light, Lovey."

"She didn't believe in unpacking, did she?"

"Doesn't look like she was planning to stay very long. I'd pack more than this for just a weekend," commented Peggy.

"I thought she was spending the winter here," said Lavinia. "Maybe she had things shipped or was going back to—where was it? Ohio?—to pick up more clothes."

They repacked Prunella's suitcase, stripped the master bed, and put on clean sheets. "I'll take these home to wash and bring them back tomorrow," said Peggy, rolling the used bed linens into a ball. "No sense running up the Murphys' utility bill."

The last rooms to be checked were the bathrooms, one up and one down. Peggy grabbed the used towels and rolled them into the sheets. Aside from the usual toiletries, a bottle of multivitamins, and a two plastic vials of prescription medicine, there was nothing out of the ordinary.

They locked the Murphys' house and prepared to head across the street to their own houses, lugging the suitcase and dirty linens.

"We went over that entire house, Lovey. And there's still one thing missing."

"What's that, PJ? I thought we got everything."

"We're still missing Prunella's pewter pill box."

"You're right. I didn't see it anywhere."

"I think when we find it, we'll know who killed her."

CHAPTER 18

PEGGY WOKE IN A TOASTY WARM HOUSE, HER head buzzing with all the things she needed to do in the week left before Thanksgiving.

Top on the list was getting in touch with Dale Hansen. In order to clear her name and get herself off Stu McIntyre's most wanted list, Peggy needed to know what was in Dale's report on Prunella Post. She also needed to get back the key Prunella had to the Murphy house.

While the coffee perked, Peggy folded the sheets and towels she'd laundered the night before.

"Mom? What's for breakfast? No more oatmeal!" Nicky made gagging sounds.

"Nicky, oatmeal is good for you."

"I hate it, Mom."

"You've made your point. How about scrambled eggs and toast?"

"All right!"

"You make the toast, I'll make the eggs."

Nicky plopped two slices of bread into the toaster, then went to the refrigerator for a glass of juice.

"It works faster if you push down the lever, honey."

Nicky made a face and pushed down the lever on the toaster while Peggy stood at the sink beating eggs in a bowl with a fork.

She was pouring the eggs into a hot skillet when the phone rang. "Nicky? Get the phone while I stir the eggs."

He zipped over and grabbed the phone. "It's for you, Mom."

"Who is it?"

"Some lady."

"Ask her to hold for a minute. Say please." Peggy stirred the eggs with quick strokes. "Butter your toast, Nicky."

Peggy scooped the creamy eggs—just the way Nicky liked them—onto a plate, handed the plate to Nicky, and reached for the phone while she picked up her coffee cup.

"Hello? . . . Missy?" Peggy put her hand over the receiver. "Nicky, why didn't you tell me it was Missy?" Nicky shrugged and kept on eating his eggs.

"Missy, where are you? London? London, England? Really? Oh, it must be beautiful. Is Ian there? No, he's not in Cobb's Landing. He's away someplace on business for Max. I don't know where he is." Peggy listened, occasionally frowning, and sipped her coffee while Missy talked. "I understand,

Missy. I'll think about it. That's all I can promise. . . .
No, I won't tell Max you called." Peggy hung up the
phone and sat in her chair, shaking her head slowly.
Et tu, Missy?

"Is anything wrong, Mom?"

"No, Nicky, everything's fine. You'd better hurry
or you'll be late for school."

The phone rang again. This time Peggy answered
it. Lavinia. "Morning, Lovey. . . . I told Nicky to
hurry. Do me a favor? When you're at the hospital,
will you see if you can get the Murphys' key from
Dale Hansen? The one we gave to Prunella. I want
that key back in our hands as soon as possible. . . .
Great. Talk to you later."

Peggy turned to Nicky. "Get a move on. Lavinia is
driving you and Charlie to school today and she's
ready to leave now."

While Nicky ran to brush his teeth and get his
school books, Peggy sat picking at the remnants of
scrambled eggs and thinking about Missy's phone
call. Was one day really so much to ask? She knew
that Missy meant well, and had risked Max's wrath
by calling, but Peggy resented the lengths Max
would go to in order to get his own way. It wasn't
only Max—although there was no denying he was
the instigator—it seemed that from the very moment
Peggy put her Thanksgiving plans out in the uni-
verse, events conspired to spoil those plans. But in
her heart, Peggy blamed Max and only Max.

"Bye Mom. I'll be home late. I've got to rehearse
for the pageant after school."

Peggy hugged her son, watching while he flew out

the front door. She waved at Lavinia and Charlie, then went back into the kitchen for another cup of coffee.

Although Peggy hated to admit it, Missy was right when she had said, "Peggy, you're the mayor of Cobb's Landing. You have to do what's good for the town, even if it means personal sacrifice."

"But I don't have to like it," Peggy muttered into her coffee cup, her chin sticking out a wee bit more than usual.

"That stubborn little chin of yours will get you in trouble, Peggy Jean," her father used to say, tapping her chin gently with his finger. It was from her father that Peggy had learned how to stand up for herself, but her mother taught her how to turn defeat into victory. "If they ever run you out of town, Peggy darling, just do the cakewalk and pretend you're leading the parade." It took awhile for Peggy to understand what that really meant—she thought cakewalk had something to do with baking until she looked it up in the dictionary—but then she knew her mother was saying, "If life gives you a lemon, make lemonade."

Peggy put her cup down on the kitchen table and threw up her hands. "What am I going to do with all the food Lovey and I bought?" She looked at the ceiling as if expecting to see the answer magically appear. Then Peggy smiled. One good thing. She wouldn't have to shop for Christmas dinner. The makings were already in her freezer.

Peggy felt her mother's gentle kiss warm on her cheek as she ran upstairs to get dressed.

CHAPTER 19

THE SNOW HAD STOPPED DURING THE NIGHT.
The sun was shining brightly, and the roads were clear
as Peggy headed out of town for the discount grocery
store to stock up on makings for mulled cider. She'd
passed the old cemetery at the Cobb's Landing town
limit when she heard a siren behind her. Looking in her
rearview mirror, she saw the police cruiser approaching, lights flashing, siren screaming. Peggy obediently
pulled over, as far as she could without ending up in a
snow bank, to let the cruiser pass.

Stu pulled up behind Peggy. He got out of the
cruiser and approached her car. "You were told not to
leave town without letting me know."

"What? Stu, give it a rest. I'm not on the lam. I'm
going to the grocery store. I'll be at the hardware
store in an hour. We can talk then."

"I'll be timing you," said Stu, looking at his

watch. "If you're not there in an hour, I'm putting out an APB on you."

Peggy reminded herself to call Dale Hansen the second she got to Tom's Tools. Within the hour, she'd done her shopping; lugged jugs of apple cider, bags of spices, and boxes of paper cups into her storeroom; lettered a sign that read *Happy Thanksgiving! Hot mulled cider—$3* for the front door of the store; had the first batch of cider warming; and was ready for business.

Precisely on the hour, the phone rang. "Tom's Tools. . . . Yes, Stu, I'm here. This is not a recording. Have a nice day." Peggy hit the disconnect, then waited for the dial tone and called Dale Hansen.

"I was just about to call Stu McIntyre," said Dale. "He dropped off that turkey skewer from your store late yesterday afternoon. It's not even close to a match. The one he brought in is brand new. The one in Prunella Post's back is much older and slightly discolored. You'll see when you get my report, I'll attach a photograph."

"When will we get your report?"

"I'll shoot for later this afternoon. The snow put me behind. I spent most of the yesterday shoveling my driveway."

"Dale, did you find any keys on the body? I'm looking for a house key."

"Yes. There was one. In a little zipper pouch hanging around her neck. Can you describe it further?"

Peggy thought for a moment. "It's on a small metal ring. Attached to it is a round plastic tag stamped with the letter *M*."

"That's it."

"Would you mind giving it to Lavinia Cooper? She'll be stopping in your office this morning during her shift. Dale, keep this between us, okay? That key belongs to the Murphy house, where Prunella was a tenant. But her rent check bounced and we need to get that key back. Lavinia and I are taking care of the house for the Murphys while they're away."

Dale's laugh echoed in Peggy's ear. "Her check bounced? Oh, that's a good one. Sure, I'll give the key to Lavinia. She can sign for it and I'll put it in my report."

Stu McIntyre entered Tom's Tools as Peggy was getting ready to hang up. "Hold on, Dale. Stu's here. Tell him what you just told me about the skewer." Peggy handed the phone to Stu.

When Stu finished talking to Dale, he turned to Peggy with a sick smile. "Well, Peggy Jean. What can I say?"

Peggy was tempted to make Stu eat crow, but she bit her tongue.

Stu cleared his throat as if he still had that furball problem. "How about this: You're off the hook. You're no longer a suspect."

"Thank you, Stu. You don't know how relieved I am to hear you say that. How about a cup of mulled cider? On the house. Then you can do something for me."

"I'll pass on the cider. What I need is coffee. I'll grab a cup at Clemmie's. What do you want me to do?"

"Lavinia and I packed up Prunella Post's belongings last night." Peggy reached in her purse for a sheet of paper. "Here's a list of everything we found. Her suitcase is in my car. I want you to store it at the police station until someone claims it."

"That's fair. Thanks, Peggy. I meant to get over to the Murphys' last night, but, ah, I was waiting for some reports to come in by fax. Well, I better go. Let's get that suitcase."

Free at last of Prunella Post, Peggy turned with a lighter heart to the business of running her hardware store.

As she was filling her cider urn for the second time, Peggy heard a voice behind her. "Look, Dad, it's the same lady we saw when we were here last time. But she's not wearing that dorky hat anymore."

Peggy recognized that voice immediately. Sure enough—it was the same boy in the blue-and-white striped T-shirt who'd been such a pain during the Colonial Village opening weekend the previous spring. Instead of a T-shirt he now sported a blue-and-white striped sweater under his navy ski jacket. The dorky hat he referred to was part of Peggy's Colonial Village costume, designed by Missy, and it looked like a ruffled shower cap. As much as she had grown to like Missy, Peggy still hated that blasted hat.

"I don't know why we came back to this dorky town. There's nothing to do here."

The father smiled somewhat apologetically. "His school closed early for Thanksgiving vacation. Problems with the heating plant."

Peggy could sympathize with a parent trying to

cope with a restless eight-year-old boy. But she also remembered that the boy was a precocious little trouble-maker and the father was also somewhat of a pain. In for a penny, in for a pound, Peggy thought as she plastered a smile on her face. If I'm going along with this Thanksgiving feast idea of Max's, I might as well go all the way.

"I'm Peggy Turner, the mayor of Cobb's Landing, and I grew up here. There's lots to do. You can ride in the horse-drawn sleighs, and you can go sledding on the hill near the old cemetery. If you don't have a sled, I've got some here for rent. Or, we're having a snowman-building contest on the village green. The winner gets a prize."

"What's the prize?" asked the boy.

"That's for me to know, and you to find out," said Peggy with a grin. "When you've finished your snowman, come back here to fill out the entry form. It costs five dollars to enter the competition, and that includes a souvenir photo of you and your snowman." A little voice whispered in Peggy's ear, prompting her to add, "By the way, I lost something on the green last week before the snowfall. A round gray metal box about so big." Peggy made a ring of her thumb and index finger to indicate the size. "If you find it, there'll be a reward."

"What's the reward?" asked the boy.

"Twenty dollars and a free cup of cider," said Peggy.

"That's not much of a reward," said the boy.

"It's a very small box," said Peggy, resisting the urge to put her thumbs in her ears, waggle her fingers, and stick out her tongue at the impudent boy.

The boy and his father left for the snow-covered village green. Peggy quickly lettered two more signs and attached them to her front door. One for sled and saucer rental, the other announcing the snowman competition. Then she ran off a stack of entry forms on her copy machine and piled them next to the cash register. She filled a Polaroid camera with fresh film and put it under the checkout counter.

By mid afternoon there were half a dozen snow people dotting the village green and a snowball fight was in progress. Peggy came back to Tom's Tools from photographing the latest contest entry to find a single long-stemmed red rose—the same red as Max's cherished bow tie—framed by delicate ferns and wrapped in green waxed paper on the checkout counter. Attached to the rose was a card, signed simply *Max.*

Although Peggy had mentioned the pillbox reward to everyone who came into Tom's Tools, at the end of the day no one had come to claim it.

CHAPTER 20

"PJ, YOU READY TO GO HOME?"

"In a second, Lovey. I have to close up first."

Lavinia leaned over to sniff the rose, now in a bud vase on the checkout counter. "Who gave you this? Ian?"

"Max," Peggy mumbled as she counted the change in the cash drawer. With the extra income generated by the cider sales, sled rentals, and snow-man entry fees, Peggy had cleared enough in one day to cover her expenses, pay herself a salary, and put a little money into her furnace fund. It had been a very good day at Tom's Tools.

"Speak up, PJ. I could have sworn you said 'Max' just now."

Peggy dumped the coins into her deposit bag. "I did. Max sent me the rose."

"I thought you were on the outs with Max."

"Long story, Lovey. I'll tell you in a minute. Tell me how your day went. Did you get the Murphys' key from Dale Hansen?"

Lavinia fished the key ring from her purse and dangled it in the air. "Here it is." She then pulled an envelope from her purse. "And I've got something else you'll want to see."

"What's that?" asked Peggy.

"Dale's autopsy report on Prunella Post."

Peggy grabbed the envelope. "Have you read it?"

Lavinia nodded.

"What does it say?" Peggy tore open the envelope and began skimming the pages, most of which were as incomprehensible to her as Greek. "You tell me. You're better at the medical stuff than I am."

"Bottom line? Prunella Post died of a heart attack."

"But what about the skewer in her back?"

"Dale's not sure about that. It did go through her clothes and into her back. He's having the skewer tested for poison."

"Poison?"

"Or any other substance that might have discolored the tip. But Dale says no matter what's found on the skewer, Prunella definitely died of a heart attack. And he found no traces of heart medication in her system."

"I still keep wondering what happened to her pill box."

"So do I, PJ. If she'd taken her pills, they might have saved her life."

"I offered a reward for the pill box, but so far no

takers." Peggy examined the photograph of the turkey skewers. Dale was right. The one from the hardware store window did not match the one in Prunella's back. They looked similar, but there were subtle differences in design, and the one from the store was brand-new shiny while the one used on Prunella Post was mottled and definitely discolored at the base. Peggy grabbed a package of new skewers and stuffed it into her purse to examine later.

After unplugging the cider urn and washing it for use the next day, Peggy did a quick check of the store before turning out the lights. "I have to make my deposit at the bank. You want to walk with me?"

The last gasps of twilight filled the sky with a purple-hued blue light as Peggy and Lavinia made their way down Main Street toward the Citizen's Bank. Shops were closing for the day, and as the interior lights went out one by one, the street lights came on, casting golden puddles of light like the glow of candles on the plow-banked snow. Clemmie's Cafe was still open—keeping extended hours through Thanksgiving weekend—the red-and-white checked curtains in the windows overlooking Main Street made the cafe look as cozy and inviting as the home of an old friend. As customers went in and out of Clemmie's, Peggy caught whiffs of homemade meatloaf and gravy that made her mouth water.

Lavinia laughed when she saw the snow people dotting the village green. "What inspired that?"

"An idea that came to me this morning," Peggy

replied. "Do you remember that kid from the opening weekend of Colonial Village?"

"Oh God. The one in the striped T-shirt? The one who dropped ice cream all over the floor of the sign shop? The one who wanted to use my bathroom and ruined our first cookout of the season? That kid?"

Peggy nodded.

"Don't tell me he's back."

Peggy nodded again. "He's here with his father for Thanksgiving week. Complaining because there's nothing to do in this dorky town."

"I'll give him something to do," said Lavinia with a groan. "He can count the rocks in the Rock River. That kid is a menace."

"That's when I came up with the idea for the snowman competition. I said the winner would get a prize."

"What's the prize?"

"That's the part I haven't figured out yet."

Lavinia laughed. "How about two weeks in Cobb's Landing? It would serve the kid right, but I don't think I could stand knowing he's here that long."

Peggy dropped her deposit bag in the night chute at the bank and the two women walked home as the sky turned to black and tiny stars began to twinkle overhead.

Stu McIntyre was sitting in the police cruiser in front of Peggy's house.

"We have to talk, Peggy," said Stu. "You've been withholding information from me."

"Oh, Stu, now what?" said Peggy. "I've told you

everything and you've got Dale's report. What more do you want?"

"I want you to tell me about your conversation with Emily."

Peggy stared at Stu, too stunned to speak.

CHAPTER 21

STU PLOPPED HIMSELF AT THE KITCHEN TABLE while Peggy made a tuna casserole for dinner.

"Stu, this really isn't a good time. Can't we have this discussion later?" Peggy opened a large can of tuna, drained it in the sink, then added the contents to the bubbling white sauce she'd just made with flour, butter, and canned chicken broth. She seasoned the mixture with salt and pepper, then spooned the tuna and sauce into a casserole dish.

"I can wait. Finish what you're doing."

Peggy whipped instant mashed potatoes with a fork until they were fluffy, then smoothed the potatoes over the tuna and sauce. She topped the casserole with lots of shredded cheddar cheese and put it in the oven to bake. She pulled a package of peas and carrots from the freezer and set it in the sink to thaw. Then she set the kitchen timer for ten minutes.

"When that timer goes off, your time is up, Stu. Nicky will be home soon, and I've got a lot to do tonight."

"I want to know what you and Emily talked about the other night."

"Stu, I'm not the one to tell you. Ask Emily."

"I did. She told me to ask you."

"Stu, I smell a rat. You're trying to pull that good cop/bad cop routine on me, and I'm not buying it. You should know better than that. And you should also know that anything I tell you is hearsay and not worth diddly-poop. I think it's high time you sat down and had a real heart-to-heart with your fiancée. Is Emily someone you know well enough to marry?"

Stu shook his head. "I thought I did, Peggy. Now I'm not so sure."

"That's a problem only you can solve, Stu. Go talk to her. Are you two still staying at the inn?"

Stu nodded. "Until we can find a place to live."

"I may have a solution to that problem." The timer dinged. "Time's up, Stu. Come see me tomorrow at the hardware store."

As Stu pulled away in the police cruiser, Nicky came running up the walk. "Hey, Mom. What was Mr. McIntyre doing here? Is he having dinner with us?"

Peggy hugged Nicky. "Not tonight, honey. Come tell me about your day while dinner's cooking. I made one of your favorites. Tuna casserole."

"Oh boy," said Nicky. "Did you put lots of cheese on top?"

Peggy nodded.

"Great." Nicky hung up his coat and dumped his school books on the stairs. "Mom, I've got a report due tomorrow for history class. Can you help me with it?"

"Sure, honey. I'll be glad to help. Tell me what the report is about."

"We're supposed to pretend we were at the first Thanksgiving in 1621 and write about it. We can be a pilgrim or an Indian."

"What do you want to be?"

"A pilgrim, I guess. It's sounds easier."

"Okay." Peggy thought for a minute. "Go wash up for dinner and we'll talk about it."

Nicky headed for the lavatory under the stairs.

"Not so fast, young man. Come with me."

Puzzled, Nicky followed his mother into the kitchen.

Peggy took a mixing bowl and filled it with cold water from the tap. She picked up a bar of soap from the sink and handed it to Nicky along with a dish-towel, then put the bowl of water in his hands. "Outside with you."

"Huh?"

"You're a pilgrim, Nicky. You don't think they had running water and indoor plumbing, do you?" Peggy opened the kitchen door leading to the back yard. "And don't forget to wash your face."

Nicky grinned and went outside to wash up.

While Nicky was gone, Peggy quickly set the table with steak knives, soup spoons, and the wooden bowls she used for salad when she had company. She put a candle into a holder and set it in the middle of the table, next to a plate containing two unsliced rolls of bread. The butter went back into the refrigerator. Instead of milk, she filled two mugs with cold apple juice. At each place she set a rolled-up linen dish towel.

Nicky came back inside, his face and hands clean and ruddy. He put the empty washing basin in the sink.

"What did you do with the water in the bowl, Nicky?"

"I dumped it in the snow."

Peggy shook her head. "Water is precious and has to be hauled from the creek. That water would have been saved in a barrel to be used in the garden or for laundry. Remember that next time, Master Nicky."

Nicky grinned.

"If I'd known we were playing pilgrims tonight I would have made something else for dinner, so we'll have to improvise, okay?"

Peggy put the casserole and bowl of vegetables on the table, lit the candle, then turned off the lights.

Nicky sat down and looked at his plate. "You forgot the forks, Mom."

Peggy grinned. "Pilgrims didn't have forks, Nicky. They had sharp knives they used for all sorts of things, a few spoons, and mostly ate with their hands. That's why you've got a big napkin." Peggy unrolled her dish towel and tucked it under her chin like a bib.

When Nicky had a large serving of tuna casserole and a spoonful of peas and carrots on his plate, he looked at his mother. "How am I supposed to eat this?"

Peggy handed Nicky the plate of rolls. "You might try breaking off a piece of bread and using that."

"Where's the butter, Mom?"

"We don't have a cow, Nicky. There is no milk or butter."

"Oh." Nicky quickly got into the spirit of the first Thanksgiving, using his bread and fingers, drinking his apple juice from a mug instead of a glass. When the meal was over, Nicky said, "Can we have ice cream for dessert?"

Peggy shook her head. "No cow, remember? No sugar, no milk, no ice, and no refrigeration. But I'll tell you what we can do. We'll pretend the first Thanksgiving was very cold and there was snow on the ground." Peggy went to her cupboard for a jar of raspberry jam. Taking two small bowls, she spooned some jam into each bowl and handed one to Nicky with a spoon. "Come on. We'll make our own dessert."

They went outside into the back yard to a clean patch of snow. Peggy scooped some of the snow into her bowl and mixed it with the jam until the mixture vaguely resembled sorbet. She tasted it, then held out the spoon to Nicky. "What do you think?"

Nicky tasted it, nodded his approval, then put snow into his own bowl and made pilgrim ice cream.

"The pilgrims didn't have sugar, and they wouldn't have had jam. What they did have were dried berries. For sweetening they would have used honey or maple syrup."

"I don't think I would have liked being a pilgrim, Mom."

"Why not?"

"Well, they had to work all the time. They didn't play baseball and they didn't have television."

"They didn't have a lot of things we take for granted, Nicky. They had to build their own homes, grow their own food, make their own clothes, chop wood for fires to keep warm in the winter."

"We're pretty lucky, aren't we?"

"Yes, we are. We have a lot to be thankful for this Thanksgiving." Peggy blew out the candle, turned the lights back on in the kitchen, and began clearing the table. "How are rehearsals coming for the pageant?"

"Great, Mom. It's going to be so cool. You'll be there to see me, won't you?"

"Of course I will."

"And after the pageant, Max said we're all going to have dinner together. Just like the pilgrims and Indians did." Nicky paused. "Does that mean we're not going to have our own turkey for Thanksgiving?"

"Nicky, I've been thinking about that. How would you feel if we had two Thanksgivings? We could have our own Thanksgiving dinner here on Sunday."

"With turkey and everything?"

"The works."

"Can Maria come for dinner?"

Peggy picked up the phone and called the Coopers. "Lovey, Nicky and I are talking about having an early Thanksgiving dinner on Sunday. Does that work for you? Come on over, I'll put the coffee on."

While the coffee was brewing, Peggy called the Alsop's. "Gina? It's Peggy. Nicky and I want to invite you to our house for dinner on Sunday. We're celebrating Thanksgiving early this year. . . . Of course Papa Luigi is welcome. Shall we say two o'clock? . . . Great. We'll see you Sunday."

Nicky hugged his mother. "Thanks, Mom. You're the best!"

"Now go do your homework. You've got a report to write."

Lavinia and Chuck came in the kitchen door. "PJ, having an early Thanksgiving dinner is a brilliant idea."

"I've also invited the Alsop's to join us. Papa Luigi is coming, too."

"Then we're going to need two turkeys," said Chuck. "I'll deep-fry one and you can roast the other."

"We'd better start defrosting the birds tonight if they're going to be thawed by Sunday."

When the menu had been decided, the Coopers went home. Peggy sat at the table, sipping her coffee and smiling to herself. Pie hopped up on Peggy's lap, curled into a tight ball, and began to purr. Peggy reached down to stroke Pie's soft fur and gently scratch the cat's favorite places behind her delicate pointed ears.

After all, Peggy mused, Thanksgiving was just a date on the calendar. A date that had been changed from Lincoln's proclaimed last Thursday in November to FDR's fourth Thursday. A change made to accommodate retailers who wanted extra shopping days between Thanksgiving and Christmas, back when Christmas shopping didn't begin until the day after Thanksgiving. Now it seemed the holly went up when the pumpkins came down. And who knew when the pilgrims actually celebrated the first Thanksgiving; probably in early October when the weather was still mild. In Canada, Thanksgiving was still celebrated in October.

No, the date itself didn't matter. It wasn't set in stone anywhere. What really mattered about Thanksgiving was celebrating and sharing with family and good friends.

Peggy picked up Pie, cradled the kitty on her shoulder, and went upstairs to check on Nicky.

CHAPTER 22

OUTSIDE THE HARDWARE STORE THE NEXT
morning, Peggy ran into Bob. "Hi Bob, what brings
you out so early? I thought you'd be at Clemmie's
having morning coffee with the boys. Hold this, will
you?" Peggy handed Pie's carrier to Bob while she
unlocked the door to Tom's Tools.

"Just wanted to see if your furnace was still running okay, Peggy. Slim's been busy in my welding
shop making parts for you. Should have them done
sometime tomorrow. Okay if we come by then to get
'em installed?"

"That would be great. Thank you." Peggy took the
carrier from Bob and entered the store. "If you need
anything for those parts, help yourself." Peggy
opened the carrier, and Pie jumped up on the checkout counter for a quick bath while Peggy bustled

around switching on lights and filling the urn with cider and mulling spices.

Bob looked out the front door, then at his watch. "She's late."

"Who's late?" mumbled Peggy, her attention focused on counting change into the cash drawer.

"Old Mrs. Mac. I used to be able to set my watch by her morning walk. Every morning, regular as clockwork. Even the morning it snowed, she was out at her usual time. Thought I'd bust a gut laughing when Mrs. Mac's dog chased the cat into the tree. It was a sight to see. Ask Stu's new girlfriend. She was talking to Prunella Post before it happened." Bob was interrupted by a group of tourists clamoring for entry blanks for the snowman competition and asking about sled rentals. "Gotta go, Peggy. See you."

"See you, Bob." Peggy finished counting the singles, fives, and tens and slipped them into the cash drawer, Bob's idle chatter momentarily forgotten. She turned to her customers. "Welcome to Cobb's Landing. How can I help you? Cider will be hot in just a minute."

By lunchtime Peggy was pooped. And hungry. Lavinia was working the day shift at the hospital and Peggy had been in such a hurry that morning getting the turkeys out of the freezer to defrost in the fridge that she'd forgotten to pack a lunch for herself. She unplugged the cider urn, slapped a *Back in 10 Minutes* sign on the front door and decided to walk to Alsop's Bakery to treat herself to a sandwich.

Main Street was bustling. Max's horse-drawn sleighs were clip-clopping up and down the still snow-packed street, full of happy tourists enjoying the novelty of the ride. Looking up toward the old cemetery, Peggy could make out tiny figures in colorful clothing whizzing down the hill.

Alsop's Bakery was so busy that people were taking numbers for service. Peggy clutched number forty-five as Gina called out "Thirty-three? Who has thirty-three?" She waved at Peggy, mouthing, "What can I get you?" Peggy grinned, mouthing back, "I'll wait," and held up her number. Lew and Papa Luigi were making and bagging sandwiches to go as quickly as Gina called out the orders.

To amuse herself while she waited, Peggy shamelessly but surreptitiously eavesdropped on conversations around her. "We've been to Plimoth and Williamsburg, so we decided to come to Cobb's Landing for Thanksgiving this year. It's quaint, but I'm a little disappointed. I thought everyone would be dressed in period costumes." Peggy looked down at her jeans and boots. Oops. Max was right. As glad as the residents were to be back in regular clothes again, the pseudo-colonial costumes were a big part of the appeal of Colonial Village. Peggy handed her number to a couple just entering the bakery and ran home to change. She'd wear the costume, but she'd be damned if she'd don that dorky hat ever again.

Peggy rounded the corner onto Main Street as Stu whizzed by in the police cruiser, heading toward the police station located in a building across from Alsop's Bakery. Peggy was not surprised to see Emily in the cruiser with Stu, but she was astonished to note that Emily was in the back seat behind the security grill.

Colonial costumes looked great on mannequins in a museum but were hell in real life, Peggy thought as she hitched up her long skirt and hustled toward the police station. How did those women get anywhere in a hurry?

When Peggy arrived at the station, Emily was being transferred to a county cruiser.

CHAPTER 23

"I DON'T WANT TO TALK TO YOU RIGHT NOW, Peggy Jean."

"Stu, I just saw Emily being taken away in a county cruiser. Tell me what happened. Maybe I can help."

Stu sat at his desk in the Cobb's Landing police station, a two-room portion—including a single jail cell—of the ground floor in the old building that also housed the Cobb's Landing town office. He reached for a bottle of aspirin and popped three in his mouth, swallowing them dry. Peggy grimaced as if the bitter taste were in her own mouth.

"Help?" Stu glared at Peggy. "How can you help? You're the one who kept telling me to talk to Emily. Well I did. Boy, did I get an ear full. Oh yeah, I know everything now. All about her marriage and the baby that died. Everything Emily said convinced me she'd killed Prunella Post. I had no choice but to arrest her." Stu slammed his fist on the scarred wooden desk. "I wish I'd never come back here."

"The truth about Emily's past would have come out sooner or later, no matter where you were. Coming back to Cobb's Landing didn't change anything."

"How can you say that? A week ago Emily and I were happy. If we'd stayed away, none of this would have happened."

"Stu, wake up and smell the Folger's. Prunella Post was stalking Emily. You think Prunella just happened to be in Cobb's Landing because she wanted to experience the joy of a New England winter? Guess again, Sherlock. Prunella set this up. And on top of it all, she stiffed the Murphys."

"Can you prove any of it?"

Peggy shook her head. "No, Stu, I can't. Except for the part about stiffing Gerald and Sara. But it makes sense. Prunella had a history of obsessive behavior. She stalked her own son when he was married to Emily. She moved to the same town, rented a house right across the street where she could monitor their every move. She was doing the same thing here. Somehow she found out about your plans and got here one jump ahead of you. From the minute she arrived in Cobb's Landing, Prunella Post was an accident waiting to happen. She brought out the worst in everyone she met, including me. I'll bet right now she's laughing herself silly over Emily's arrest."

"I wouldn't be too sure of that, Mayor."

"Max! Where did you come from?"

Max leaned against the doorway to the police office, right leg crossed over his left. Dangling from his
right hand was a paper bag from Alsop's Bakery. "I
just happened to be in the neighborhood and the door
was wide open."

"We were talking about Prunella Post."

"Dreadful woman," said Max, clucking his
tongue. "I knew from the first moment I laid eyes on
her that she was trouble. She got no better than she
deserved. Good riddance to bad rubbish, I say. Where
she is now she won't be needing that awful down
coat." Max chuckled at his own little joke, then held
out the paper bag to Peggy. "Your lunch, Mayor."
Max extended his left elbow. "Shall we? You've got
customers waiting. Ticktock, ticktock. Time is
money."

As they left the police station, Max turned back to
Stu. "I once promised you a wedding on the village
green and a honeymoon anywhere you wanted to go.
The offer's still good." Max winked at Stu. "Thanksgiving morning would be the perfect time for a wedding. The tourists will love it." Max paused, then
added, "I hate to bring up petty commerce at a time
like this; but, you'll have to vacate your room at the
inn. We're overbooked for Thanksgiving. Checkout
time is in one hour." With a brief wave to Stu, Max
escorted Peggy out the door and down Main Street
toward Tom's Tools.

"Max," said Peggy. "A wedding on Thanksgiving
morning? Aren't you jumping the gun? Emily's in
jail."

Max waved away Peggy's concerns with a flick of

his hand. "A mere trifle. A temporary inconvenience. Everything will be sorted out in time. Trust me."

"What do you know that I don't?"

"That's for me to know, and you to find out." Max grinned his impish little grin. "You received the rose I sent you?"

Peggy nodded. "It's lovely. Thank you." Then she stopped and looked at Max, imitating Pie's squinty-eyed stare. "Why are you being so nice? A week ago you shooed me out of your sleigh. Rather rudely, I might add."

Max flashed Peggy a look of contrition and placed his right hand on his heart. "I want to make amends." He held out the Alsop's Bakery bag to Peggy. "Accept this as a peace offering."

"You think you can placate me with a sandwich?"

"Would I be so crass? I think not." Max assumed his favored pose of injured innocence. "I was wrong—and don't ever quote me or I'll deny it to your dying day—not to consider your feelings about the holiday."

"Well . . ."

"Don't make plans for next Wednesday night. Bring Nicky with you and dress in warm clothing. You'll be outside for most of the evening. Meet me at the inn at five sharp and don't be late."

"Max, what's going on?"

Max retreated to his inscrutable, very smug and very annoying, old self.

"All right, don't bother answering. I know what you're going to say anyway." Peggy mouthed, "That's for me to know and you to find out," ending by sticking her tongue out at Max like a little kid in a schoolyard name-calling contest.

With a sly chuckle, followed a wink and a wave, Max was gone, leaving Peggy in front of Tom's Tools holding the bag from Alsop's Bakery.

CHAPTER 24

"STU'S MOVED BACK HOME WITH OLD MRS. MCIN-
tyre," said Lavinia.

"How do you know that?" asked Peggy.

Friday night the two women were in Peggy's
kitchen, preparing food for the Sunday afternoon
Thanksgiving feast. Nicky and Charlie were at rehearsal for the Thanksgiving pageant, and Chuck and
his high school shop students were busy building
scenery.

"Chuck told me. He ran into Stu at the inn this afternoon as Stu was loading his suitcases in the
cruiser."

"I'm not surprised," said Peggy. "I guess it makes
sense. He needs a temporary place to stay, and his
mother has plenty of room. I was going to suggest
that Stu and Emily rent the Murphy house, but with
Emily in jail . . ."

Lavinia sat at Peggy's kitchen table, quartering oranges for cranberry-orange relish, while Peggy sorted through the cranberries to pick out the bad ones.

"God, poor Stu," said Lavinia. "Imagine having to arrest your own fiancée."

"Stu wasn't happy about it," said Peggy. "At first he blamed me."

"Why you?"

"Because I kept telling him he needed to talk to Emily."

"Did you ever tell him what she told you?"

"You think Stu would have believed me? Not on your life. Like I said before, he would have thought I was trying to save my own hide. Stu needed to hear the truth about her past from Emily herself."

"But in this case the truth didn't set her free, PJ. It got Emily a trip to the county jail. Even though I don't like her any better, I do feel sorry for her. Imagine being in jail on Thanksgiving."

"Max thinks Emily will be out by Thanksgiving. He's offered Stu a wedding on the village green Thanksgiving morning and a honeymoon anywhere they want to go. You know Max—anything he thinks will appeal to the tourists. He's probably planning on charging admission to the wedding to cover the cost of the honeymoon."

Peggy chuckled as she went to the cupboard for her grandmother's cast-iron grinder—no Cuisinart for her—which she clamped onto the golden oak table, placing a glass bowl under the mouth of the grinder. Lavinia fed the cut-up oranges into the grinder as Peggy slowly rotated the handle, feeling the age-smoothed wood like satin in her palm.

"Remember when our mothers used to do this, Lovey?"

Lavinia smiled and nodded, lost in memories of Thanksgivings past. "I remember something else, too. You wait here, I'll be right back." Lavinia ran over to her house, returning a few minutes later with a brown paper sack. "Our mothers were always nipping at the sherry while they cooked Thanksgiving dinner. So I bought us a bottle." Lavinia went to Peggy's cupboard for two small glasses. She opened the bottle of sherry and poured a glass for each of them. "Cheers, PJ."

Peggy stopped grinding oranges to pick up her own glass. "Cheers, Lovey."

"Remember how we used to sneak sips of sherry when we didn't think they were looking?"

Peggy giggled. "But they always knew."

When Peggy finished grinding the oranges and cranberries, Lavinia reached for the sugar, adding it to the ground fruit a half cup at a time. After frequent stirrings and tastings, the relish was declared just right. Not too sweet, not too tart. Just right. Peggy covered the bowl and put it in the refrigerator.

Lavinia topped off the sherry glasses. "What's next?"

Peggy looked at her list. "Let's do the pies next. While your apple-mince is baking, we'll make my frozen pumpkin ice cream pie. Sunday morning we can chop the celery and onions for the stuffing and make the green bean casserole."

While Lavinia made pie crust from scratch, Peggy peeled and sliced the apples. Lavinia put the crust-covered glass pie dish on the table and began arranging the apple slices; after each layer, Peggy spooned a thin topping of mincemeat until the dish was full. They worked quickly on the lattice top, then put the pie in the oven to bake.

"We've got leftovers, PJ. Enough for one small tart each." Lavinia grabbed two small glass dishes from Peggy's cupboard and quickly assembled two tarts, which she then put in the oven.

Peggy cleared the table, then got out a ready-made graham cracker crust, a can of pumpkin, and a quart of cinnamon ice cream. When the pumpkin ice cream pie was made, Peggy popped it into her freezer and topped with a note for Nicky: *You touch, you die.*

While the apple-mince pies finished baking, Peggy and Lavinia cleaned up the kitchen, then sat down with their sherry.

Peggy got up and went to a kitchen drawer.

"Now what, PJ?"

"I thought I'd get out all the spoons, basters, and things we'll need for roasting the turkey so I don't have to dump out drawers Sunday morning looking for them." Peggy rummaged through the drawer, pulling out a flat cardboard box.

"What's that, PJ?"

Peggy looked at the box, put it on the table, then went for her purse. She pulled out the envelope with Dale Hansen's report, then dug into her bag for the package of turkey skewers she'd taken from Tom's Tools.

First Peggy took the photograph from Dale's report showing the two skewers side by side and put it on the table. Then she opened the crumbling cardboard box. "These were my mother's turkey skewers. She had them for years and years." She pulled a skewer from the box, took a new skewer from the package, and laid the two side by side.

They were virtually identical to the skewers in Dale's photograph, down to the discoloration on one skewer.

Lavinia picked up the old skewer and examined it carefully. "That's not blood or poison like Dale thought. Only a woman would know the real answer. That discoloration was made by years of heat-baked turkey juices. No matter how hard you scrub, the stain will never come off."

Peggy grinned. "The box says six skewers, and I've got all six right here. So, the one used on Prunella Post came from someone's kitchen."

"That could be any kitchen in Cobb's Landing," said Lavinia. "No one here ever throws anything away."

CHAPTER 25

BOB AND SLIM WERE IN TOM'S TOOLS FOR THEIR ritual Saturday morning free coffee. "We got those furnace parts done, Peggy. We can go over and put them in now. Okay with you?"

Peggy called Nicky to tell him Slim and Bob were on the way, then turned to Slim. "Leave your bill. I'll have the cash ready when you get back."

"I hear Stu's girlfriend was arrested," said Bob. "Like I told you yesterday, Peggy Jean, I saw her talking to the Post woman on the green that morning."

"How do you know it was Stu's girlfriend? You sure it wasn't a tourist?"

"Nah. That was no tourist. I recognized her dark green coat. Saw her walking with Stu a couple of days before that. Sure looked like she and the Post woman were arguing. I was in my truck heading for

Clemmie's, so I couldn't hear what was actually being said, but they were pretty mad about something. Funny, both of them being new in town and all. Wonder what they'd have to be so mad about."

Peggy let Bob's idle speculation hang in the air. As much as she wanted to pump Bob for more information, Emily's past wasn't her news to broadcast.

"C'mon on Slim, let's get over to Peggy's. We want to get this done before the football games start." The men tossed their empty foam cups in the trash barrel and headed out.

Peggy tried to remember what Bob had told her the day before. The little voice in her head said it was important, but she couldn't for the life of her remember what it was.

The weather had stayed cold and the village green was undergoing a population explosion of snow people. Peggy finally decided first prize was a twenty-five dollar gift certificate to Tom's Tools. Seemed only fair that she provide the prize if she was raking in the profits from the competition. She filled the Polaroid with more film and ran off extra entry blanks.

Then she opened Slim's bill. Hmmmm. She didn't have enough cash on hand to cover it, even though the cost of repairs was far less than buying a new furnace. Peggy put her *Back in 5 Minutes* sign on the door, wrapped her woven woolen shawl tightly around her shoulders—she'd wear the colonial costume through Thanksgiving weekend, then it was going straight back into mothballs until spring—and headed for the ATM at the Citizen's Bank.

Max emerged from the bank as Peggy was slipping the folded bills into the pocket of her starched linen apron.

"Don't you believe in writing checks, Mayor?"

"Good morning to you, too, Max. I just wanted some cash."

"Do you need a loan? I can offer very attractive interest rates."

"Max! Do you cross-examine everyone who uses your cash machine?"

"Only those who take out two hundred dollars at one time."

"Max! You are a snoop! There must be a law against that."

"Poop on silly laws." Max grinned. "You know my motto: 'It's not who you know, it's what you know about them.' Are you sure you don't need financial help?"

"I'm fine, Max. Really."

"I'll walk back to the hardware store with you. It's not smart to carry that much cash."

"Max, I'm not five years old."

"I've been thinking about our police department," said Max as they walked up Main Street. "Now that Cobb's Landing is becoming a prosperous little tourist attraction, it's only natural to see an increase in crime."

"Here? In Cobb's Landing? You can't be serious. This is a small village where everyone knows everyone else."

"Not any longer." Max gestured to the tourists building snowmen on the green. "Do you know those

people? Can you tell me their names?" When they
reached Tom's Tools, Max looked at the new store
window Peggy had just paid for. "When was the last
time you had a broken store window?"

Peggy thought for a minute. "Never, until this
week."

"My point precisely. We need more police presence. We'll discuss it at the next town meeting. Put it
on the agenda." With a wink and a wave, Max was
gone.

Standing at the door of the hardware store was old
Mrs. McIntyre, her gloved hand clutching Poopsie's
leash. "Fine way to run a business, Peggy Jean
Turner. I've been standing here longer than five minutes." Old Mrs. McIntyre stared pointedly at the sign
on the door.

"I'm back now," said Peggy, unlocking the door
and holding it open for Mrs. McIntyre to enter. "How
about a nice cup of hot mulled cider? My treat."

Pie heard Poopsie's high-pitched yapping and immediately bounded from the checkout counter where
she'd been dozing contentedly to a top shelf, where
she sat hunched, eyes narrowed to slits, ready to hiss,
the fur on her normally sleek back raised to an angry
ridge.

"Mrs. McIntyre, would you mind tying Poopsie
up outside?"

"In this cold? I certainly will not. You shouldn't
keep animals in a retail store. It's against the law."
Mrs. McIntyre sniffed as she helped herself to a cup
of mulled cider.

The corner's of Peggy's mouth twitched as she bit

back a sharp retort. Putting on her best smile, she said instead, "How can I help you today?"

"Now that my Stu is home again," old Mrs. McIntyre practically purred her only son's name, "I'm going to cook him a real old-fashioned Thanksgiving dinner." Mrs. McIntyre pulled a shopping list from her pocket and handed it to Peggy. "These are the items I need. I got rid of my old things when Stu went away and I had only myself to cook for."

Do I look like a personal shopper? thought Peggy as she picked up a basket and began piling in the items on the list, beginning with long-handled wooden spoons and a turkey baster.

Old Mrs. McIntyre stood near the cider urn, feeding bits of a fresh baked corn muffin to Poopsie while she sipped free hot cider.

"That muffin was my breakfast," muttered Peggy as she dropped a package of turkey skewers into the basket.

While Peggy whizzed around Tom's Tools, her long skirt swishing bell-like from side to side, consulting the list and adding things to the basket, Mrs. McIntyre cooed to Poopsie. "Oh Poopsie, now that Stu's back home we're going to be a real family again. I'll make dinner for him every night just like I did when he was in school. We can go for walks together every morning. The three of us. It'll be like old times, just you wait and see."

Peggy's eyes widened as she listened to old Mrs. McIntyre, but she kept her mouth clamped shut. When she got back to the checkout counter, she tallied the items in the basket. "That'll be $75.84, Mrs. McIntyre."

"Put it on my account."

Peggy pointed to the *No Credit* sign hanging behind the checkout counter. "We don't have accounts here, Mrs. McIntyre. I'll gladly take cash, a check, or a credit card."

"I left home without my purse. I'll send Stu to settle with you later." Old Mrs. McIntyre reached for the shopping bag containing her purchases.

A smile still plastered to her face, Peggy swept the bag off the counter out of old Mrs. McIntyre's grasp. "I'm sure Stu will be glad to bring these things home for you after he's paid your bill. Have a lovely day, Mrs. McIntyre, and thank you for shopping at Tom's Tools."

With a haughty lift to her head, Mrs. McIntyre sailed out of the store, Poopsie trotting obediently behind her.

Peggy chuckled to herself in celebration of her minor victory as she set the bag behind the checkout counter. It wasn't often that anyone bested old Mrs. McIntyre and lived to tell about it.

When they were gone, Pie crept down from the top shelf and settled back on the checkout counter to resume her nap.

A faint rustle reminded Peggy of the money secreted in her apron pocket. She reached for Slim's invoice, quickly recounted the money she'd gotten from the ATM, and wrapped the bills inside. As she opened the cash drawer to put the money away until

Slim's return, she heard Bob's voice echoing in her head, telling her what he'd seen that morning on the green. Was it possible he'd witnessed the prologue to a murder? Peggy grabbed a cup of coffee and settled on her high-backed stool to think.

CHAPTER 26

LAVINIA POPPED INTO TOM'S TOOLS EARLY SATurday afternoon. "You closing early today, PJ? The guys are all at our house watching football. Nicky's there, too. I couldn't stand being in the same house with all that noise, beer, and testosterone. I don't know how I'm going to last through the Super Bowl. Football season seems to drag on longer every year. Why can't they watch something nice and quiet, like golf?"

Peggy smiled. "I thought I'd stay open until three; it's been a busy day so far. Then I'm going to check out the latest entries in the snowman competition. You want to go over to the green and take pictures of the new ones while the light's good?" Peggy handed Lavinia a list of snowman entries and the Polaroid camera. "I started numbering them, we've got so many. Take two pictures of each—one for the bulletin board and one for the contestant. Here's an extra package of film."

The front door banged open. "I wanna build another snowman, but a better one this time. Do I hafta pay again?" It was the boy in the blue-and-white striped sweater. He stopped short when he saw Lavinia Cooper staring at him like hawk eyeing a tasty rodent. "I remember you from last time," the boy said in a small voice. Lavinia never cracked a smile.

Before Lavinia could commit an act that would land her a jail cell next to Emily's, Peggy smoothly intervened. "I'll tell you what. It's Freddy, isn't it?" The boy nodded. "Freddy, since you were the first to enter the competition, you can have one do-over. But, you have to choose which snowman is your official entry. Is that fair? You let me know before we judge the entries Tuesday afternoon."

Freddy ran out of Tom's Tools, letting the door slam shut behind him.

"Time has not improved his manners," commented Lavinia dryly. "You put up with this sort of thing every day? I don't know how you do it." Lavinia picked up the camera. "Don't blame me if that kid ends up face down in the snow. I'll bring you a picture." Lavinia grinned and left the store.

The Cobb's Landing police cruiser was double-parked outside when Stu McIntyre ran in. "I've come to pay Mom's bill." Stu handed Peggy a check for the exact amount owed. Peggy slipped the check into the cash drawer and handed Stu the shopping bag.

"What is all this stuff? Mom doesn't need any more kitchen things. She still has the spice rack I made her in eighth grade shop class. She never throws anything out."

"Your mother said she's making an old-fashioned Thanksgiving dinner for you. She seems really glad to have you home."

Stu rolled his eyes. "Some homecoming. I was hoping to have my Thanksgiving dinner with Emily. Peggy, do me a favor? Emily's wants to see you. Would you have time to visit her this afternoon? It would mean a lot to me."

Peggy sighed, then nodded.

"Can you be there by four? I'll call the county jail. Tell Emily I love her."

Peggy nodded again. Stu waved his thanks as he ran back to the cruiser.

"Why am I doing this?" Peggy said aloud. "The last thing I want to do is trot my happy self to the county jail for a visit with a woman I hardly know."

"PJ, have you lost it?" Lavinia put the camera on the counter along with a stack of prints. "You're talking to yourself. That is not a very good thing."

"It's only bad if I start answering," said Peggy with a smile. "Stu was just here. He asked me to visit Emily at the county jail this afternoon, and like a spineless wimp I said yes. Why did I do that?"

Lavinia grinned. "Because you are a spineless wimp. But a lovable one. And Stu is our friend. He's practically family. Tell you what. I'll drive. I need an excuse to stay away from the house until football is over. Let's get a move on. I hope you're planning on changing clothes first."

Peggy shut down Tom's Tools for the weekend,

getting her bank deposit ready, loading Pie into her carrier. She did one last check, making sure the cider urn and coffee pot were unplugged and washed. The she flipped the sign from OPEN to CLOSED and locked the door.

The orange prison jumpsuit may have been perfect for a Thanksgiving theme, but it was the worst possible color for someone with Emily's pale skin and blonde hair. She appeared sapped of all energy, reduced to an ashen wraith.

"Peggy, thank you for coming. I know you're doing this for Stu, not me, but I'm glad you're here. I need a friend."

"Stu asked me to tell you he loves you."

Emily's blue eyes sparkled and a smile lit her face.

In that moment Peggy saw in Emily the woman Stu had fallen in love with, the one with whom he wanted to spend the rest of his life.

Then Emily looked around the barren visiting area. Tears welled in her eyes. "How did everything go so wrong?"

"Emily, get a grip. We need to talk about what happened the morning Prunella Post died. I know you were on the green. You were seen talking to Prunella, and it looked like you two were having an argument. What was all that about?"

"Prunella was ranting again about how I'd ruined her son's life. And how she wouldn't rest until she'd made me as miserable as I had made her. It was the same thing she always said."

Peggy nodded sympathetically. "Prunella was dangerously unbalanced. I picked up on that the first day we met. She was obsessed, consumed by her own misery."

"Peggy, you have no idea. I thought I'd finally gotten away from her when Stu and I came to Cobb's Landing. It was my worst nightmare come to life to find her here waiting like a poisonous spider lurking in a web."

"What did you say to her?"

"I asked her to go away. To leave me in peace."

"What happened?"

"She laughed at me."

"Is that why you went to the village green that morning? To confront Prunella?"

Emily shook her head. "I had no idea Prunella would be there. I went to meet Stu's mother."

"Really? Why?"

"Stu told me his mother went for a walk every morning with her little dog."

"Was this a prearranged meeting?"

Emily shook her head. "I hadn't even spoken to his mother. I was hoping to meet her for the first time that morning. I wanted to tell her how much I loved Stu and that I wanted to make him happy. I wanted her blessing."

That'll be a cold day in hell, thought Peggy as she looked at Emily's sincere face. What you don't know is that old Mrs. McIntyre isn't going to part with her only son any easier than Prunella Post did. "What happened?"

"I got up early and left the inn while Stu was still asleep. It was so quiet and peaceful. I love walking when it's quiet. I could hear the birds chirping in the trees, the water in the river splashing on the rocks. The fresh snow was so pretty. Everything looked like a fairy tale."

Until the sisters grim arrived to spoil everything, thought Peggy. "Then what happened?"

"First Prunella arrived with her horrid cat."

"Wait," said Peggy. "I want to make sure I've got this all straight. Where were you?"

"I told you, at the green."

"You came from the inn. You walked up Main Street?"

"That's right. Oh, I see what you mean. You want to know where everyone was and when."

"Exactly."

"Well, I was on Main Street, on the sidewalk, looking at the green."

"And Prunella came from where?"

"From behind me. From the direction of your house."

"Prunella was renting the Murphy house across the street from mine."

"The first thing I saw was Holstein. He streaked past me onto the green. Then Prunella came, calling to that wretched cat. When she saw me, she started screaming at me."

"You two were where?"

"On the sidewalk. On Main Street. Then I spotted Mrs. McIntyre approaching from the far side of the green."

"How did you know it was Mrs. McIntyre?"

"I assumed it was. She was walking a little dog and called it Poopsie."

"What did you do?"

"I ran away from Prunella along the side street toward Mrs. McIntyre."

"And then?"

"Mrs. McIntyre let Poopsie off the leash. Poopsie spotted Holstein in the middle of the green and started barking. Then he chased Holstein up a tree. Prunella started yelling for Holstein and ran onto the green toward the dog. When that happened I ran to the far side of the green and hid in the pines."

"And?"

"When I looked back, Prunella was lying face down in the snow."

"Where was old Mrs. McIntyre?"

"I don't know. She and the little dog had vanished. Then I heard Stu calling for me, so I stayed hidden in the pines. Then I saw you standing on Main Street looking at the green and Stu coming toward you."

"You stayed hidden in the pines the whole time?"

Emily nodded. "I was too afraid to move. Then you left and came back, and the ambulance came and a man in a car. I knew then that Prunella was dead and I could be blamed for it. When the ambulance left I ran back to the inn and was in the dining room when Stu found me."

"Did you see anyone else? Did anyone else see you?"

Emily thought for a minute. "Wait! There *was* someone. A man drove by in a tow truck while I was talking to Prunella. Just before the dog chased the cat up the tree."

That jibes with what Bob said, thought Peggy. Unfortunately, it doesn't clear Emily. It's still possible that she's responsible for Prunella's death. If only Ian were here. I'd ask him what to do. "Have you got a lawyer?" asked Peggy.

Emily shook her head. "Not yet. I don't know anyone here to call."

"You keep your mouth shut," said Peggy. "Don't talk to anyone else, including the police, without having a lawyer present. I know someone who may be able to help you."

CHAPTER 27

"WHY SO SILENT, PJ?" LAVINIA ASKED ON THE drive from the county jail back to Cobb's Landing.

"I was just thinking about Emily," replied Peggy. "She's our age, Lovey, and look how different we are. You and I have led such safe, secure lives. We live in the town where we grew up. We live in the same homes where we grew up. We married our high school sweethearts. How predictable is that?"

"Your point?"

"Emily's life is different. She's a . . ." Peggy paused to think. "A risk taker. I don't know where she grew up, or if she has brothers and sisters. I really don't know much about her. But I do know she's got guts, and I admire her for that. It takes courage to do what she's done. I just wonder if, under similar circumstances, you and I would have been as brave."

Lavinia snorted. "Brave? Some would call it

damned foolhardy, PJ. Can you imagine leaving your life for some guy you met on the Internet? We know Stu; we know he's a nice guy. But for all Emily knows, he could be another Ted Bundy. A lot of people thought Ted Bundy was a nice guy. He was personable, charming, and a serial killer. A woman's got to have a screw loose to get hooked up with a guy like that. Someone she doesn't even know."

"I still think what Emily did took guts. She was willing to put everything on the line for love."

"Yeah. And look what it got her. Don't you think if she could turn back the clock she'd rather be back in Ohio teaching school than in jail in Cobb's Landing?"

"Oh, Lovey, that's not the point. She didn't expect to end up in jail. And I'm not sure she deserves to be there."

"You think she's innocent?"

"I don't think she was responsible for Prunella's death."

"If not Emily, and not you, then who?"

"I don't know," said Peggy. "And that bothers me. I can't get a clear picture of what happened the morning Prunella died. It's all bits and pieces and there's a big chunk missing. Max said today now that Cobb's Landing is becoming a prosperous tourist attraction we're going to see an increase in crime. He says we need a bigger police force."

"Max is a fine one to talk. He's the one who got us into this Colonial Village thing in the first place."

"But we all went along with it, Lovey. We can't blame Max for leading us astray like the Pied Piper with the innocent children. Before Max came along, Cobb's Landing was dying. Economically we're a lot better off than we were six months ago."

"I agree with you on the money part. But I don't like having to lock my house every time I leave or yelling at Charlie because he forgot to lock up if he went out after school. I liked it better when we all knew and trusted each other. When I could be in my back yard enjoying a barbeque without some brat in a blue-and-white striped T-shirt yelling over my fence about using my bathroom. Call me provincial, PJ, but I liked our safe and secure life. And that's the kind of life I want for Charlie."

Peggy sighed. "That's what I want for Nicky, too, but we may be living in a fool's paradise."

They reached the outskirts of Cobb's Landing as the last light left the sky. Lavinia slowed down near the old cemetery. They looked down at Cobb's Landing. At the streetlamps illuminating the horse-drawn sleighs clip-clopping along Main Street, the twinkling lights in the little Cape Cod houses set in orderly rows on parallel streets named after trees and birds. They saw the snow, looking bluish white in the fading light, the wood smoke rising from chimneys, and in the far distance, the dark ribbon of the Rock River. The two women breathed sighs of pure contentment. There was no place like home.

"Want to grab a pizza at Alsop's for dinner?" Lavinia asked. "We've got a lot to do to get ready for our Thanksgiving feast tomorrow."

"First, I want to go to the inn. I need to see Max."

"What for?"

"He's the only one who can help save Emily."

Lavinia found the last open spot in the inn's parking lot. As they walked toward the red brick building that was the former button factory, Lavinia glanced at the license plates on the cars and SUVs. "I'll say this for Max, PJ, he certainly has a flair for promotion. Look at all of those out-of-state cars. Who would have thought so many people would want to leave their homes to spend Thanksgiving in Cobb's Landing?"

They walked down the winding cobblestone path to the inn's entrance. Through the glass-paned double doors they could see the bustling reception area on the left, the crackling fire in the large stone fireplace on the right, and the inn's guests sitting in comfortable upholstered love seats and wing-back leather chairs, having drinks and gazing at the floodlit Rock River and the continual splash of cascading water from the water wheel. The river-dampened air smelled of pine and wood smoke.

Peggy went up to the reception desk and asked for Max.

"I'll ring his room for you. How have you been, Peggy?"

"Fine, Barbara. How about you?"

"Great. I really love working here. Oh, Max, Peggy Turner is here to see you. She's with Mrs. Cooper." Barbara hung up the house phone and turned to Peggy. "Max will be right down, Peggy. He asked you two to have a drink—on the house—while you wait." Barbara beckoned to a passing waiter. "These ladies are Max's guests for drinks."

The waiter escorted Peggy and Lavinia to seats near a large picture window overlooking the river. "What can I bring you ladies?"

Peggy hesitated. It wasn't often that she went out for a drink. In Cobb's Landing most people did their social drinking at home and when they drank it was beer or an occasional highball, or perhaps a glass of wine.

"Perhaps you'd like to see our specialty menu?" The waiter handed them small printed drink menus. "The house drink for Thanksgiving is called a Cranberry Bog. It's cranberry juice, club soda, and vodka, with a splash of Cointreau. You can have it frozen or on the rocks."

"I'll have one frozen," said Peggy.

"Make that two," said Lavinia.

The waiter returned with their drinks and a bowl of warmed mixed nuts. Lavinia sipped her drink and began picking the cashews out of the nut bowl. "I could live like this, PJ. How about you?"

Peggy nodded and continued sipping her drink. "You know, Lovey, this drink is really good. If we did some of the prep work tonight, we'd have time to run to the store tomorrow morning and we could have Cranberry Bogs before our own Thanksgiving dinner. Do you suppose the waiter will give us the recipe?"

"He'll do more than that," said Max. "He'll carry the ingredients to your car. With my compliments."

"Max! You don't have to do that," said Peggy.

"Nonsense, Mayor. It's a small recompense for all the coffee I've consumed at your store. Please allow me to do you this little favor."

"Thank you, Max. We're having an early Thanksgiving celebration at my house tomorrow afternoon. Will you join us?"

Max actually blushed. "That's the first time I've been invited to anyone's home in Cobb's Landing. But that's not why you came here to see me. What can I do for you?"

Peggy leaned forward and began talking to Max in a low whisper about Emily. Max listened intently, nodding from time to time, glancing frequently at his watch.

"Max, am I keeping you from something?" asked Peggy. "I didn't mean to barge in on your evening."

"Not at all," said Max. "It's just that I have some pressing business and am waiting for my ride. I'm sorry I won't be able to attend your dinner tomorrow, but I'm touched that you thought of me."

The sound of Max's helicopter was heard, then subsided as it landed.

"Excuse me, ladies," said Max. "I really must go." He gestured to the waiter. "Another round for the ladies. Later I'll want you to take a box from the bar to their car." He turned back to Peggy and Lavinia. "Enjoy your drinks." Max left the inn and went out to the parking lot.

"Peggy, we really should be getting home," said Lavinia. "Chuck will be wondering where I am."

"Go call him from the receptionist desk. And while you're at it, call Alsop's and order our pizza," said Peggy, sipping her fresh drink. Sitting here in the inn, looking at the fire and sipping a drink she'd never had before, made her feel like a pampered tourist. She looked in the bowl of nuts, but Lavinia had eaten all the cashews. Peggy nibbled on a smoked almond and watched the water tumbling off the water wheel.

Then Peggy felt a soft kiss on her cheek and smelled the very familiar scent of a spicy aftershave.

"Ian! Where did you come from?"

Ian smiled and pointed skyward. "Air Max. He told me you and Lavinia were in here having drinks. I tried calling your house an hour ago, but there was no answer. I've missed you, Peggy."

Peggy smiled and reached for Ian's hand. "Welcome home. I've missed you, too. I've got so much to talk to you about. I need your help."

"Max already briefed me, but you can fill in the details later."

"Ian! Fancy meeting you here," said Lavinia, returning to the table. "When did you get back? Are you having pizza with us? PJ, I'll call Alsop's back and have them make an extra pie." Lavinia U-turned back to the phone at reception.

"What can I get you, sir?" asked the waiter.

"An extra dry vodka martini. Shaken not stirred," replied Ian with a smile. "Peggy, give me five minutes to change. I'll be right back." Ian picked up his briefcase and headed for his room on the second floor of the inn.

CHAPTER 28

WHEN THE PIZZA WAS REDUCED TO ITALIAN-spiced crusts that Lavinia insisted on cubing and adding to the turkey stuffing, Chuck and Peggy stood at the sink cleaning the two defrosted turkeys that would be cooked the next day. Lavinia cooked the giblets while Ian chopped celery and onions.

"How about filling me in on what's happened while I've been away?" Ian looked at Peggy affectionately. "I go away for a week and you're in trouble again."

"Peggy can take care of herself," said Chuck.

"Maybe you should stick around more often," said Lavinia.

"Wait a minute!" said Peggy. "I'm not the one in trouble, and I can speak for myself."

The Coopers smiled.

"Prunella Post is dead," said Peggy.

"So I heard," said Ian.

"Emily has been arrested," said Peggy. "She's in the county jail."

"Who's Emily?" asked Ian.

"Stu's fiancée," said Lavinia. "Ian, you do remember Stu?"

"Of course I remember Stu," said Ian. "I haven't been away that long, and I wasn't in a coma. Stu was the police chief when I came to Cobb's Landing, then he left and is back again in his old job. I didn't know there was an Emily involved."

"No one else did either," said Peggy. "Especially old Mrs. McIntyre. Stu called before he came home and asked me to break the news of his engagement to his mother."

"Stu's a grown man," said Ian. "Surely he can speak for himself."

"Not where his mother is concerned," said Lavinia. "Old Mrs. McIntyre is a tyrant."

"Can someone put these events in chronological order?" said Ian. He put aside the bowls of chopped celery and onions and picked up a pad and pen Peggy had on the table for making lists. Lavinia set the pan of giblets aside to cool. Chuck put the turkeys back in the refrigerator and passed around cold bottles of beer.

"You left on Monday," said Peggy. "Tuesday morning Prunella Post was discovered, face down in the snow, on the village green."

"When did Stu get back?"

"Monday. Just before you left. He and Emily were in my store. I invited them to my house for dinner

Monday night and went home to get dinner started.
When I came back you were waiting to say goodbye."

"And Prunella Post was still alive?" asked Ian.

"Was she ever," said Lavinia. "Prunella and that
wretched cat Holstein. Prunella stormed into my
house like the thirteenth fairy at the christening and
cast an evil spell on the entire evening."

"I thought the dinner was here," said Ian.

"It started out here," said Peggy, "until Holstein
flew in through the front door and Pie made a sham-
bles of my kitchen. Then we moved the party to the
Cooper's house."

"That's when Prunella appeared," said Lavinia,
"and threatened Emily."

"Why would Prunella threaten Emily? I thought
they were both strangers in Cobb's Landing," said
Ian.

"Prunella was Emily's former mother-in-law,"
said Peggy.

Ian's eyes widened. "Really?"

"Prunella Post was one sick ticket," said Peggy.
"When Emily was married to Prunella's son Alan,
their baby died under mysterious circumstances one
night while Prunella was babysitting. Emily had a
nervous breakdown, and when she got out of the hospital, Alan had filed for divorce at Prunella's insis-
tence. Then Alan died in an auto accident, which
Prunella blamed on Emily."

Ian held up his hand to stop Peggy's narrative
while he made some notes.

"Was Emily driving when Alan died?" asked Ian.

"No, apparently Alan was drunk driving and had an accident. Prunella twisted the whole thing around to blame Emily because, according to Prunella, Emily had ruined her son's life. Just as she also blamed Emily for the death of her infant son, even though Prunella was alone in the house with the baby when he died. Emily was convinced that Holstein was somehow involved. She said she found cat hair in the crib."

"The old wive's tale about cats sucking the air out of babies," said Lavinia. "If Prunella Post were still alive I'd want to kill her myself."

"Emily said it was no secret that she hated Prunella," added Peggy. "Prunella had a real talent for bringing out the worst in everyone she met. The night she ruined my dinner party I yelled in front of witnesses that I wanted to kill her. Of course I wasn't serious, but unfortunately, Stu was one of those witnesses. For a while I was his leading suspect, if you can believe it."

"You were?" Ian was incredulous. "On such flimsy evidence? I thought Stu had a better grasp of police investigative techniques."

"There was something else," said Peggy. "A turkey skewer was found sticking out of Prunella's back. And my store window was broken about the time of Prunella's death. Missing from the Thanksgiving window display was a turkey skewer."

"But the one in Prunella's back wasn't the brand new skewer from PJ's window," said Lavinia. "It was an old one, slightly different design, discolored from years of use. You'll probably find them in every kitchen in Cobb's Landing. I've got a set in my own kitchen drawer. They belonged to my mother."

"When did Emily become the leading suspect?" asked Ian.

"When she finally told Stu about her past relationship with Prunella," replied Peggy.

"They're going to be married and he didn't know about Emily's past?" asked Ian.

"They haven't known each other very long," said Peggy.

"They met on the Internet," said Lavinia.

"Really?" Ian scribbled more notes. "Where? In a chat room?"

"No, through an Internet dating service," said Lavinia. "Can you imagine? That's like buying a pig in a poke. They never even met in person until about three weeks ago."

"That's fast work, even for Stu," commented Chuck.

"Max offered Stu a wedding on the green Thanksgiving morning with a honeymoon anywhere they want to go," said Peggy.

Ian's mouth twitched. "Max has a flair for showmanship. He learned it from P.T. Barnum."

"Wasn't it Barnum who said 'There's a sucker born every minute'?" asked Chuck. "I wonder what Max takes us for?"

"Max has a very deep attachment to Cobb's Landing," said Ian. "Now tell me what happened the morning Prunella Post died."

"Peggy was the only one there," said Lavinia.

"Not exactly," said Peggy. "There was one other witness, but I'll get to that part in a minute."

"Take it away, Peggy," said Ian.

"It had snowed the night before," said Peggy. "It was Tuesday morning and I was walking to the store to open up. I spotted something orange on the green and walked over to look. There, in her brown coat and orange hat, was Prunella Post lying in the snow. At that point Stu came up. He was looking for Emily. We didn't know if Prunella was alive or dead. I went to the hardware store to call the ambulance and discovered my store window was broken. I went back to Stu at the green and we waited for the ambulance. Dale Hansen, the medical examiner, followed the ambulance in his car. Dale said Prunella was dead. His follow-up report stated that she died of heart failure."

"She had a history of heart disease," said Lavinia. "She always carried a pillbox of heart medication with her."

"The pillbox was never found," said Peggy. "Stu searched the snow on the green, Lavinia and I cleaned her belongings out of the Murphy house, Dale checked all the clothes Prunella was wearing that morning. I even offered a reward, but no one came to claim it."

"Why was Stu looking for Emily?" asked Ian.

"Stu and Emily were staying at the inn. Stu said he woke up and Emily was gone, so he went out looking for her. When he finally got back to the inn after Prunella's body was taken away in the ambulance, Emily was in the dining room having breakfast. She told Stu she'd gotten up early and gone for a walk."

"But that wasn't true?" asked Ian.

"Partially," said Peggy. "Stu asked me to visit Emily at the county jail this afternoon and it was then that I heard Emily's story. She got up and went for a walk because she wanted to meet old Mrs. McIntyre. Stu had told her that Mrs. McIntyre always walked her dog early in the morning. When Emily arrived at the green, Prunella Post appeared and the two had an argument. Bob—from the garage; he and Slim have been working on my furnace—saw the argument when he drove past the green in his tow truck, and he told me about it yesterday when he was in the hardware store. But I was too busy counting change and wasn't paying attention. Then he brought it up again this morning. Bob also mentioned that he saw Poopsie, Mrs. McIntyre's dog, chase Holstein up a tree. Emily says when that happened she ran away from Prunella to the far side of the green. When she was hidden in the pines she looked back and saw Prunella lying in the snow, but Mrs. McIntyre and Poopsie were gone."

"So there were no witnesses when Prunella died?"

"Only Holstein. He was up a tree. Claudia Lewis and I got him down later that morning with three cans of tuna."

"Where is the cat now?" asked Ian.

"He's still with Claudia until someone comes to claim him. If not, I think Claudia may keep him. They seem to get along," said Peggy.

"What about Prunella's next of kin?"

"I don't think there are any," said Peggy. "According to Emily, Prunella was a widow and Alan was her only son."

"I'll do some checking," said Ian. "Peggy, do you feel like going for a walk?"

"At this hour?" said Chuck.

"I'd like to see where Prunella was found," said Ian.

Lavinia kicked Chuck under the table. "PJ, Nicky's already at our house watching television with Charlie. He can spend the night." Lavinia got up and tugged on Chuck's sleeve. "Come on Chuck, let's go home. You have to get your deep-fryer ready for your Cajun turkey. PJ, we'll see you tomorrow. What time is dinner?"

"I told the Alsop's two, which means we'll eat about three."

"Perfect," said Lavinia. "I'll be over here about ten to help you stuff the bird." She turned to her husband. "Say good night, Chuck."

"Good night, Chuck." Laughing, Chuck took Lavinia's hand and led her out of Peggy's kitchen door.

Peggy turned to Ian. "Were you serious about going for a walk?"

"Why not?" said Ian. "It's a beautiful night, and I'll finally have a chance to be alone with you."

Peggy grinned and ran to get her coat and boots.

Arm in arm, Peggy and Ian strolled over to Main Street. Cobb's Landing had settled down for the night, most of the homes dark. In the distance they heard a church bell bong eleven times. Main Street was completely deserted, all businesses closed for the evening. At Clemmie's a dim light glowed behind the red-and-white checked curtains, casting a rosy glow onto the snow-splotched sidewalk.

They approached the village green, and the spot

where Peggy stood the morning Prunella was discovered face down in the snow. A slightly less-than-half moon, pale orange against the blackened sky, hung in the air like a cocked smile, illuminating the snow people with a ghostly light.

"Good God," said Ian. "What are those?"

"I organized a snowman-building competition," said Peggy. "Something to keep the tourist kids occupied."

Ian hugged Peggy. "You are a marvel. Max should be taking lessons from you."

"Wait," said Peggy in a whisper. She held a gloved finger to her lips. "Shhhhh."

Ian whispered in Peggy's ear. "Why are we whispering?"

"Because," Peggy whispered back, "there's someone out there on the green. Look."

As they watched, a shadowed figure moved between the snow people, toppling them one by one. Ian put his hand on Peggy's shoulder, indicating she should stand still, then he sprinted onto the green, catching the intruder in the act.

"You're hurting me, let go!" said a young voice.

Peggy ran onto the green, where Ian was holding the youngster's arms in a firm grip. Peggy recognized the navy ski jacket and looked into the face of Freddy, the boy in the blue-and-white striped sweater. "It's almost midnight. Does your father know where you are?" asked Peggy.

"No, he's asleep," said Freddy.

"And that's exactly where you should be. Are you staying at the inn?"

The boy nodded.

"And why were you out here knocking over snowmen?"

"Because I wanted to win the contest," said the boy defiantly.

"You're a poor sport, Freddy. And you're disqualified."

"You can't do that," wailed Freddy.

"Oh, yes, I can," said Peggy in her no-nonsense voice, one that made Nicky snap to attention immediately. "It's my contest and I make the rules. You're out. And I'm going to tell your father why. Let's go."

With Freddy between them, Peggy and Ian marched to the inn. They went to the reception desk, where Ian used the house phone to call Freddy's room. A few minutes later, his father—in bathrobe and slippers with sleep-tousled hair—came down the stairs from the second floor. He looked somewhat confused to see his fully dressed son with Peggy's arm firmly clamped around his shoulders.

"We found your son on the village green a few minutes ago, knocking down snowmen because he wanted to win the competition. Freddy has been disqualified, and I thought you should know why," said Peggy. "I suggest you keep an eye on your son. Even in Cobb's Landing we don't let our children run around unsupervised after dark."

Freddy's father mumbled his thanks and an apology for his son's behavior, then led his somewhat subdued son up the stairs. When they reached the landing, Freddy turned and stuck his tongue out at Peggy while making a rude gesture with his free hand.

Peggy sighed and shook her head. "That boy has juvenile delinquent written all over him."

"Cheer up, Peggy," said Ian. "With any luck he'll grow up to be fine upstanding citizen, or"—Ian winked—"a politician." Ian looked around the empty first floor sitting area where the fire had died to glowing embers. "I was going to offer you a drink, but I see the bar's closed. I do, however, have an excellent bottle of brandy in my suite. Will you join me?"

Peggy thought about it for a fleeting second, then smiled and walked up the stairs with Ian.

CHAPTER 29

PEGGY WALKED HOME IN THE LIGHTLY FALLING snow, swinging a bag of pumpkin muffins from Clemmie's Cafe.

She unlocked the front door of her house, humming a merry tune under her breath, as the grandfather clock chimed eight. She hung up her coat and went to the kitchen to start a pot of coffee. A few minutes later there was a tap on the kitchen door. There stood Lavinia in her robe and slippers.

"Just getting home, PJ? That was some walk." Lavinia grinned at her best friend.

Peggy felt her cheeks begin to flush.

"PJ, your secret's safe with me! Everyone is my house is still asleep." Lavinia laughed as she helped herself to a cup of coffee. "The only reason I know you didn't come home last night is because there are only one set of tracks on the walk leading to your front door and it's been snowing for several hours."

"You win a pocket for your spy coat," Peggy said with a smile. "Have a muffin and wipe that Cheshire Cat grin off your face."

"Well? Dish, girl!"

"Lovey, didn't your mother ever teach you not to talk with your mouth full?"

Peggy put butter and a knife on the table and poured a cup of coffee for herself.

Lavinia reached over to pat Peggy's hand. "PJ, I know how long it's been since Tom died. It's about time you had a night off from being a full-time mother, mayor, and business woman. Why do you think I had Nicky spend the night at our house?"

"Ok, Lovey, I owe you one. Have another muffin!" Peggy slid the bag toward Lavinia after taking a muffin for herself. "What are you doing up so early anyway?"

"Chuck wanted his turkey out of your refrigerator. You know how fussy these Emeril wannabe's can be. He says he needs to season and marinate the bird this morning before he starts up the deep-fat fryer." Lavinia went to the refrigerator and took out one the turkeys resting in foil roasting pans. "I'll run this home for Chuck and be right back. Then I want details!"

"I don't kiss and tell," said Peggy with a smile. "But I have some dirt you're gonna love hearing."

Lavinia was back before Peggy had finished her first cup of coffee. "Tell me!"

"It's about that brat in the blue-and-white striped

sweater. I don't think he'll be bothering us much longer. We caught him on the green last night." Peggy paused for a swallow of coffee.

"What was he doing?"

"Knocking out the competition," said Peggy. "The kid was so desperate to win the snowman contest he was knocking down all the snow people."

"If I ever caught Charlie behaving that way, he wouldn't be able to sit down for a week," said Lavinia.

Peggy nodded. "Ian and I hauled him back to the inn and I had a talk with his father. The kid snuck out after his father went to sleep." Peggy shook her head. "I think Max is right. We're not a sleepy little village any longer. We need more police presence. I hate to think what could have happened to that kid, wandering around on his own in the middle of the night."

"Let's get a move on, PJ. We've got company to feed in a few hours. I'm going home for a quick shower and to get dressed. I'll be back in about half an hour. Do you need anything?"

"I can't think of anything right now."

"How could you? Your head's still in the clouds." Lavinia hugged Peggy. "I'm so glad you're happy. You deserve it. See you in a bit."

As Lavinia went out the kitchen door, Nicky ran in. "Hi, Mom. What's for breakfast? Charlie and I want to go sledding."

Peggy hugged her son. "Nicky, don't ever start a conversation by asking 'What's for . . . ?' Women really hate that question. The answer is: whatever you feel like fixing for yourself. You're old enough to make your own breakfast. There are pumpkin muffins and butter on the table. You know where the juice and milk are. I'll be right back." Peggy left a dumbfounded Nicky standing in the kitchen as she went upstairs to her bedroom to change.

When she returned to the kitchen, Nicky was slurping milk, pushing a spoon around a bowl of cereal, and had a buttered muffin ready to eat. His empty juice glass sat on the table.

"Don't forget, Nicky. Today's our special Thanksgiving dinner for family and friends."

"What time is Maria coming?" Nicky's eyes sparkled when he said Maria's name.

"I told the Alsops to come over about two, honey. We'll probably eat around three."

"Okay, I'll be home before two, Mom." Nicky got up from the table and headed out of the kitchen.

"Not so fast, Nicky. You forgot something." Peggy pointed to the breakfast dishes still sitting on the table. "Cleared, rinsed, and put in the sink, please."

"Okay, Mom. I forgot." Nicky cleared his dishes off the table, then, in an effort to be extra helpful, wiped the table, brushing the crumbs onto the floor. "Can I go now?"

Peggy smiled, but said nothing about the crumbs on the floor that now needed sweeping. That lesson would come another day. "Go have fun, honey."

Lavinia came in the back door, brandishing a VCR tape. "Look what I've got! It's last year's Macy's parade. I'll put it on and we'll pretend it's really Thanksgiving morning. I've already bought a new tape that we'll use to tape this year's parade while we're at the pageant. I know it won't be the same as seeing it live, but it'll be better than not seeing it at all."

Peggy preheated her oven to roast the turkey while Lavinia got out the ingredients for the stuffing. Together they mixed the celery and onion Ian had chopped with the cubed pizza crusts and packages of stuffing mix.

"I know some people like to get fancy with stuffing, adding things like chestnuts or oysters, but I always keep mine simple," said Peggy. "It's the same as my mother always made."

"My mother, too," said Lavinia. "It's what Chuck and Charlie like. Don't mess with a good thing."

As they were stuffing the twenty-pound turkey, Chuck ran into the kitchen. "Peggy, I've got a crisis. I forgot to get that injector thing."

"Do you mean a larding needle?"

"No, that big syringe-type thing you fill with the liquid seasoning and inject into the bird. Have you got one?"

"Not here, but there's one left at the store. C'mon, we'll go and get it. For you, I'll open up on a Sunday."

Peggy and Chuck ran over to Tom's Tools. The injector was exactly where Peggy knew it would be, and it was the last one in stock. Peggy scribbled a note to herself and put it on the checkout counter. Chuck handed Peggy a five-dollar bill. "Will that cover it?"

"Sure. Is that all you need? I won't have time to come back here again today."

When they got home, Ian and Lavinia were putting the turkey to be roasted into Peggy's oven.

"Ian, have you ever deep-fried a turkey?" asked Chuck.

"No, but I've read about it. You need a big kettle, propane, and lots of hot oil. And you want to cook it outside, so the house doesn't catch on fire."

"Come with me," said Chuck. "This is the first time I've deep-fried a turkey and I need an extra pair of hands."

Ian stopped long enough to kiss Peggy—and whisper to her that Freddy and his father had checked out of the inn that morning—before heading out the back door for the Coopers' kitchen.

While Peggy peeled enough spuds to make her feel she was on permanent KP, Lavinia prepared her sweet potato casserole topped with mini-marshmallows.

"What's left, PJ?"

"The green bean casserole. I'll take care of that." Peggy got out condensed mushroom soup, a large package of frozen green beans, and a container of French fried onion rings. Soon the casserole was ready for the oven.

"Let's go over and check on Chuck," said Lavinia. "Then we'll come back and clean up this mess."

They found Chuck and Ian in the living room, bottles of cold beer in their hands, watching the football pre-game show.

"If this isn't a typical Thanksgiving," said Lavinia with a mock groan. "Where's this turkey I've been hearing so much about?"

"It's resting," replied Chuck, his eyes still fixed on the television.

"What did it do? Run the hundred-yard dash?"

Chuck grinned. "It'll be done on time, honey. It only needs an hour to fry. What time is dinner?"

"The Alsops are coming at two, we're eating at three," said Peggy.

"I'll put it in the oil at one thirty. That's an hour from now."

"Come on, PJ," said Lavinia. "Let's go back to your house. It tires me to see two grown men working so hard."

Lavinia stopped to grab two cold beers from her refrigerator. "We need sustenance while we do dishes."

They stood at Peggy's kitchen sink—Peggy washing, Lavinia drying—while in the background the Rockettes kicked their way through a Christmas medley.

"Every year I say I'm going to buy a dishwasher," said Peggy. "And every year something comes up. This year it's the blasted furnace."

"I know, PJ," said Lavinia, setting the clean dishes on the kitchen table to be put away later. "I say the same thing. A dishwasher is the one appliance I wouldn't mind seeing under the Christmas tree. But when Chuck gave me an electric frying pan for our first anniversary I yelled so much that he's never given me another appliance. He says if I want anything like that I can buy it myself."

Peggy let the soapy water run out of the sink and wiped her hands on a dish towel. "There. That's done." She opened the oven to peek at the turkey.

"Oh, that smells good," said Lavinia, reaching for the baster. "Let me baste it. I always loved doing that when I was a little girl."

"Have at it, Lovey. I'll put these dishes away."

"There are going to be how many for dinner?"

Peggy stopped to count. "Five of us and four Alsops. No, wait there are six of us. I forgot to count Ian. That's ten total."

Lavinia grinned. "That'll be our little secret, PJ."

"You get so used to being single," said Peggy, "you forget what it's like to be part of a couple again."

"Is Ian the one?"

"Could be, Lovey. But I don't know how Nicky feels about it. I guess we'll have to wait and see."

"Don't wait too long. Nicky will be ready for college before you know it. Then where will you be?"

"I don't want to become one those mothers who never lets go of her son. Prunella Post really scared me. And look at old Mrs. McIntyre. They're two of a kind. Women who never made a life for themselves."

Lavinia smiled. "PJ, you're the last woman anyone would ever say that about. You have more lives going than a cat. I want you to be happy. If Ian's the one, I'm all for it. Promise me one thing."

"What's that?"

"I get to be the flower girl."

Peggy laughed and swatted Lavinia with the dishtowel. "Now, Lovey, how are we going to feed everyone? If only the weather were warm, we could eat outside. But that's not possible. I'm thinking we'll put all the food out on the kitchen table and let everyone help themselves, then we can eat in the living room. If it were just us, I'd put the leaves in the table, like we did when we were kids. But ten is just too many to seat at this table. What I wouldn't give for a dining room. Just for today."

"And what would you do with a dining room the rest of the year? Fill it with junk? Use it for a box room?" Lavinia thought for a minute. "How about putting the adults at this table, then we can set up a smaller table for Nicky, Maria, and Charlie? I've got a folding table and chairs at home. I'll run and get them. We can always have coffee and dessert in the living room after dinner."

Peggy cleaned off her kitchen counters to make room for the serving dishes, then put the leaves in her golden oak table. She covered the table with her mother's cherished linen cloth and began setting the table with her mother's good silver and china.

Nicky came in, his cheeks rosy from sledding. "That turkey sure smells good. Can I peek at it?"

"You can peek, but no picking. It's not done yet."

Nicky peeked at the turkey, then ran upstairs to change for dinner. "Tell me the minute Maria gets here, okay?"

The Alsops arrived promptly at two, bringing fresh baked bread and rolls and bottles of Papa Luigi's homemade wine. Lew and Papa Luigi went over to the Cooper's to see how Chuck and Ian were making out with the deep-fried turkey, while Maria huddled giggling with Nicky and Charlie.

Gina joined Peggy and Lavinia in the kitchen. Lavinia got out the sherry bottle and poured a glass for each of them. "When Peggy and I were kids, our mothers always drank sherry while making Thanksgiving dinner. It's tradition."

Peggy pulled the turkey from the oven, its skin roasted to a golden brown.

"What can I do, Peggy?" asked Gina.

"How are you at mashing potatoes? Use the electric mixer; it's on the wall. If you do the potatoes, I'll make the gravy."

Lavinia giggled. "Don't forget the turkey droppings, PJ."

"The what?" asked Gina.

"Turkey droppings. It's an old family joke. One Thanksgiving Peggy's dad said he was making gravy with turkey droppings. He really meant drippings."

"You two are so lucky to have grown up together," said Gina. "You have so many shared memories. Thank you for making us part of your family today."

"We're glad you're here," said Peggy. "Thank you for bringing the lovely bread and rolls. But you didn't have to bake on a Sunday just for us."

"We bake seven days a week, even though the bakery is only open Monday through Saturday. We make all the baked goods for the inn and Clemmie's."

"You mean those pumpkin muffins I bought at Clemmie's this morning were yours?" said Peggy.

Gina nodded. "I thought you knew. Well, don't let on that I told you. Especially to Max. He likes to brag about his pastry chef at the inn."

Peggy grinned. "I won't tell. But I love knowing something secret about Max."

"We always make our deliveries early, before anyone else is up. About the only one Lew or I ever see is old Mrs. McIntyre out walking her dog."

"Did you see her the morning Prunella Post died?"

Gina thought for a minute. "Yes, I was driving that morning. Coming back from the inn, I saw them both."

"Gina, sit down. Tell me what you saw," said Peggy.

"I was driving back from the inn. It had snowed, and Main Street was slippery, so I was driving slowly. I saw Prunella Post standing in the snow talking to old Mrs. McIntyre. Mrs. McIntyre had her back to the street. Poopsie was running around them, barking so loud I could hear it though my closed car windows. Then the car started to skid and I forgot all about it until now." Gina looked at Peggy. "Is it important?"

"I don't know, Gina. But just to be safe I wouldn't mention it to anyone else."

As Gina bent her head to sip her sherry, Peggy and Lavinia exchanged a long wondering look.

CHAPTER 30

WITH THANKSGIVING ONLY THREE DAYS AWAY, Peggy was busier at Tom's Tools than the proverbial one-armed paperhanger. Word of Chuck's delicious deep-fried turkey had spread through Cobb's Landing and suddenly everyone wanted to try it. By two that afternoon Peggy was completely sold out of Cajun cooking equipment and begging her supplier for a special delivery before Thanksgiving.

The mulled cider urn had been refilled so many times that Peggy had lost count.

As Peggy was getting ready to close for the day, Stu McIntyre walked into the hardware store. He looked like he hadn't slept in weeks. His handsome rugged face was haggard, and there were deep black circles under his eyes. He pulled two sealed plastic bags from his parka pocket and placed them on the checkout counter.

"Do these things look familiar to you?"

Peggy picked up the first bag. Inside was a box of turkey skewers, but one was missing from the set. The box was the same sort of crumbling cardboard box that Peggy had in her own kitchen drawer. The set that had belonged to her mother. The remaining skewers in the bagged set were discolored from years of use.

In the second bag was a small, round pewter pill-box.

Peggy looked up at Stu. "Where did you find these things?"

"I'd rather not say right now, Peggy Jean. Do they look familiar?"

Peggy nodded. "If the inside of the pillbox lid is engraved with the initials PP, that's Prunella Post's pillbox."

"I thought as much," said Stu with a sigh. "What about the skewers?

"It looks like a match to the one in Dale Hansen's photograph. But I can't be sure until I look at the photo again, and that's at home."

"Can I give you a lift home, Peggy?"

"If you don't mind stopping at the bank first, so I can make my deposit," Peggy replied. "Wait until I put Pie in her carrier."

Stu picked up the cat and held her close. Pie stretched her neck and Stu rubbed his fingers lightly under her chin. Pie closed her eyes and purred. "You forget Pie and I are old friends. You've taken good care of her."

"She's in the store with me almost every day. The

Tom's Tools resident cat." Peggy opened the carrier and Stu gently placed the cat inside. "She likes going home because she knows it's dinner time."

After a quick stop at the bank, Stu pulled the police cruiser up in front of Peggy's house and parked.

"You hungry?" asked Peggy. "It's turkey leftovers. I think we'll be eating leftovers for a week."

Stu shook his head. "Maybe later, Peggy. But I sure could use a cup of coffee."

"Come in. I'll put on the coffee while I look for the photograph."

Nicky was sitting at the kitchen table munching on a turkey sandwich and drinking a glass of milk. "Hey, Mr. McIntyre. Are you here for dinner?"

Stu high-fived Nicky. "Not tonight, Nicky. I need to talk to your mom. Grown-up stuff."

"Nicky, take your sandwich and milk up to your room. You can start on your homework. I'll call you when dinner's ready."

"I've got Thanksgiving rehearsal tonight, Mom. That's why I made my own sandwich. I'm going to ride with Charlie and his dad." Nicky looked up at the clock. "Gotta go in five minutes. We get to try on our costumes tonight."

"Then stay here and finish eating, honey. Is one sandwich enough for you?"

Nicky grinned. "I made two. I already ate the first one. Can I have a piece of pumpkin ice cream pie for dessert?"

"You certainly may." Peggy turned to Stu. "Would you like a piece of pie with your coffee?"

"That sounds good."

Peggy got the remains of the frozen pumpkin pie out of the freezer and cut two pieces. There was just enough left for her to eat later. She topped the pie with aerosol whipped cream and set the plates before Stu and Nicky.

When Nicky had left for rehearsal, after a reminder from Peggy to brush his teeth and remember to take his house key, she found the photograph that Dale Hansen had taken and sat at the table with Stu.

The old skewer in the photo was an identical match to the set Stu had sealed in the plastic bag.

Stu sighed, exhaling slowly, then he put his head in his hands.

"Stu? Are you all right?"

Stu looked at Peggy and shook his head. "I need to ask a favor, Peggy Jean. A big one. I promise this will be the last one."

Peggy smiled. "Stuart McIntyre, don't make a promise you can't keep. You and I will be asking each other for favors for years to come. What can I do?"

"Take a ride with me. I need a witness."

"Now?"

"Now. Please?"

"You want to tell me what this is all about?"

"Not yet. Okay?"

"Okay. Give me five minutes to feed Pie and Buster and I'll be ready to go."

Stu finished the last of his coffee and picked up the plastic bag containing the turkey skewers and put it back in his pocket. "I'll meet you outside."

After a short ride, Stu pulled up in his mother's driveway and parked the cruiser.

"You want me to wait here for you, Stu?"

"No, Peggy. I want you to come inside with me. Please?"

A knot began to form in Peggy's stomach. She got out of the car and walked with Stu up the freshly shoveled sidewalk.

Old Mrs. McIntyre was peering through the curtains as they reached the front door. She opened the door, then stood wiping her hands on her apron. "Wipe your feet on the outside mat, Stu. I don't want you tracking snow in my house. You didn't tell me you were bringing Peggy Jean home for dinner. I wish you'd let me know these things in advance. You know I dislike surprises. You're late. You know I always like to eat dinner at six on the dot."

Stu looked at his mother. "Sit down, Mother, and shut up. You and I have things to discuss."

"Stuart McIntyre, I didn't raise you to talk to me like that. You will apologize this instant."

Keeping his unbuttoned parka on, Stu walked into the overfurnished living room. Peggy hadn't been in old Mrs. McIntyre's house since Stu was a boy. The room was overheated and stuffy. The furnishings were what Peggy vaguely remembered. Heavy dark furniture with crocheted doilies on the head and armrests, cabinets filled with knickknacks, faded photographs in frames on the wall. It wasn't a room for relaxing; it was a room to sit with your feet together and to speak when spoken to. No wonder Stu had spent most of his school years hanging out at his friends' houses.

Stu sat on the edge of a chair, his feet firmly planted on the floor. "I said sit down, Mother."

Peggy remained in the doorway to the living room, wishing she were somewhere else. Anywhere but here.

Old Mrs. McIntyre sat. She glared at her son, her thin lips pressed firmly together. Poopsie ran into the room, yapping. The little brown dog looked at Stu, then at old Mrs. McIntyre, then ran from one to the other, yapping, yapping in a high-pitched bark that gave Peggy an instant headache.

Stu looked at the little dog. "Sit."

Poopsie sat close to old Mrs. McIntyre and began to quiver.

Stu reached into his parka pocket and pulled out the two plastic bags, which he held by his fingertips, one in each hand. "Do these things look familiar, Mother?" Stu's voice was low and steely.

Old Mrs. McIntyre's eyes opened wide. "Where did you get those things?"

"I found them in a drawer in the basement."

"I've told you before not to go poking into things that don't concern you. You have your own room. You keep your things there. The rest of the house is mine."

"Do these things look familiar, Mother?"

"I don't know what you're talking about. I've never seen them before."

"I think you have."

Mrs. McIntyre started to rise from her chair. "I won't sit here in my own house and be talked to this way by my own son."

"Sit down, Mother."

Mrs. McIntyre sat.

Stu continued. "If I have these items dusted for prints, what do you think I'll find?"

"I'm sure I wouldn't know."

"Your prints, Mother. I'll find your prints. Your prints on Prunella Post's pillbox."

Mrs. McIntyre's face crumbled like soft wax falling from a melting candle.

"Why will I find your prints? And what was Prunella Post's pillbox doing in a drawer in your basement?"

"Her horrid cat attacked my Poopsie."

At the sound of its name, Poopsie began to yap. Stu pointed a finger at the dog and it stopped barking.

"You stood there on the village green and let Prunella Post die because her cat attacked your dog?" ask Stu.

"You weren't there, Stu. You don't know." Mrs. McIntyre sat up straight, filled with righteous indignation. "Peggy Jean, you saw it happen. Tell him. The attack on Poopsie was completely unprovoked. Why, Poopsie had to stay overnight in a strange place while that horrible cat was tested for rabies. You can still see where Claudia Lewis had to put stitches in poor Poopsie's little head."

"Your dog is still alive. Prunella Post is dead. That makes you an accessory to murder."

Mrs. McIntyre began to sputter. "Why, why, I never touched the woman."

"Then how did one your old turkey skewers end up in Prunella Post's back? Answer that, Mother."

"I, I, I was carrying it with me for protection."

"Protection against what?"

Mrs. McIntyre clamped her lips together and refused to answer.

"I'll tell you what happened, Mother. You delib-
erately provoked Prunella Post that Tuesday morning
on the village green. You wanted to get even for
what her cat had done to your dog. And when she
had a heart attack, after your dog chased her cat into
a tree, you stood there watching. We know that
Prunella Post always carried her pillbox with her
and it was full of her heart medication. She probably
wanted you to open it and give her one of the pills
that would have saved her life. But you stood there
and did nothing. Then you took the pillbox with you
and hid it in the basement, thinking that no one
would ever find it."

Mrs. McIntyre's face lost all color, her lips took
on a faintly bluish cast.

"You were wrong to ask me to clean the basement
for you, Mother. And you were wrong to sit back and
let Emily take the blame for something you had
done."

"Emily's not good enough for you. You belong
here with me. Prunella Post deserved to die for what
her cat did to my Poopsie. I'm not sorry she's gone."

"I'm a grown man, Mother. Whether or not I
marry Emily is none of your concern. But I'll tell you
one thing, I'll never spend another night under your
roof."

Mrs. McIntyre's hand clutched her heart.

"Don't pull that same old crap, Mother. You're as
strong as ox. You'll outlive everyone. And you'll
continue to bully them to their dying days."

Mrs. McIntyre slumped forward in her chair.

"Stu, I'm calling the ambulance," said Peggy, reaching for the phone on the table in the hallway. "I think your mother really is having a heart attack."

Poopsie began to yap and tried to jump into old Mrs. McIntyre's lap. Peggy hung up the phone.

"Stu, the ambulance will be here soon. Does your mother take any medication? Where will I find it?"

"Mother doesn't believe in doctors. She's never taken anything stronger than an aspirin in her life."

By the time the ambulance arrived, it was too late. Old Mrs. McIntyre was dead.

CHAPTER 31

PEGGY AND IAN WERE SITTING AT PEGGY'S kitchen table eating turkey sandwiches when Lavinia tapped on the back door.

"PJ, I was at the hospital tonight when the ambulance brought in old Mrs. McIntyre's body. I can't believe she's dead. She was too mean to die. I thought she would outlive us all."

"You want a turkey sandwich, Lovey? Help yourself. The makings are all here on the table. I'll get you a plate."

Lavinia sat down and began making herself a fat turkey sandwich on the leftover bread from Alsop's Bakery. "How's Stu taking it? Is he all right?"

"Not so loud, Lovey. Stu's asleep on my living room couch."

Lavinia clamped her hand over mouth. "Sorry. I didn't know. What's he doing here?"

"He needed a place to sleep and he didn't want to be alone tonight. I was going to let him use Nicky's room, but Nicky has school tomorrow. Stu refused to sleep in my room—said he didn't want to put me out—so he's got the couch."

"Poor Stu," said Lavinia. "What a rotten homecoming. First his fiancée ends up in jail, then his mother dies. I wouldn't blame him if he took off again."

"That's not going to happen. Stu's home to stay. There is a happy ending. Emily's being released from the county jail first thing tomorrow morning." Peggy glanced fondly at Ian. "Ian's already taken care of the paperwork, but it was too late tonight to get it processed."

"Really? They found out what happened to Prunella Post?"

Peggy nodded. "Stu put it all together."

"Don't keep me in suspense, PJ. What happened?"

Peggy looked again at Ian. He put his arm around the back of her chair as Peggy began to talk. "Stu came to see me in the hardware store as I was closing up today. He had two plastic bags with him. One held a box of old turkey skewers. Like the ones you and I have from our mothers. In the other bag was Prunella Post's pillbox."

"My God," said Lavinia. "Where did Stu find those? In Emily's luggage?"

Peggy shook her head. "No. Emily had nothing to do with Prunella's death. Stu found those items in a drawer in old Mrs. McIntyre's basement."

"How did they get there?"

"Lovey, you need nourishment. The blood has seeped out of your brain. Maybe you also need some ginkgo biloba. Max says it's good for memory loss."

Lavinia made a face at Peggy.

"Lovey, the skewers and the pillbox got into the basement drawer because old Mrs. McIntyre put them there. After she watched Prunella Post die."

Lavinia smacked her forehead with the palm of her hand. "Holy crap. Old Mrs. McIntyre. Who would have guessed. Why?"

"Because Prunella's cat Holstein attacked Poopsie."

"Sheesh. Talk about family feud. I can't believe it. It was so trivial. Animals get into fights all the time."

"It wasn't trivial to Prunella Post or old Mrs. McIntyre," said Ian. "Those pets were their surrogate sons. All those women had in their lives were their pets." Ian's slipped his arm around Peggy's shoulders and leaned over to plant a quick kiss on her head. "When Prunella's cat attacked Mrs. McIntyre's dog it became a personal issue. Especially to old Mrs. McIntyre, when her dog had to spend the night at the vet's while Holstein was quarantined for possible rabies."

"When Gina said yesterday that she'd seen Mrs. McIntyre talking to Prunella Post on the green, I knew that Mrs. McIntyre was more involved than she was admitting," said Peggy. "I called Stu this morning and hinted that he might want to have a talk with his mother. Then Stu came by with the skewers and the pillbox but wouldn't tell me where he found them."

Lavinia put her half-eaten sandwich down on the plate. "I can't eat another bite until I've heard the whole story."

"Stu and I came over here to compare the skewers he had in the bag with the one in Dale Hansen's photograph. They were a perfect match. Then Stu asked me to go on a ride with him. He said he needed a witness. We ended up at his mother's house."

"Good grief," said Lavinia.

"Old Mrs. McIntyre was her usual bullying self when we arrived. But, Lovey, you would have been so proud of Stu. For the first time in his life he stood up to his mother. She finally confessed the whole thing. Stu was smart enough to get the entire conversation on tape. And I was there and heard every word. Prunella Post may have died of a heart attack, but it was old Mrs. McIntyre who withheld the medication that might have saved her life. As Stu said, that made Mrs. McIntyre an accessory to murder."

"How did Mrs. McIntyre die?" asked Lavinia.

"Stu told her that whether or not he married Emily, he wouldn't spend another night under his mother's roof. At that moment Mrs. McIntyre had a heart attack and died on the spot."

"You live by the sword, you die by the sword," Lavinia said softly.

The three sat at the table in silence.

Lavinia reached for a piece of tissue and began dabbing her eyes. "This is so silly, but suddenly I feel like crying. And I never even liked old Mrs. McIntyre."

Peggy nodded. "I know exactly how you feel.

Cobb's Landing won't be the same without her. I
don't think I'll ever be able to look at the village
green, especially in the early morning, without expecting to see old Mrs. McIntyre walking Poopsie."

Ian reached for a piece of tissue and handed it to
Peggy. Peggy wiped the tears from her eyes.

"Poopsie. What happened to Poopsie?" asked
Lavinia.

"Claudia Lewis has him," said Peggy.

Lavinia smiled through her tears. "Poor Claudia. I
hope her kennel is big enough. We should give her a
pair of those noise-canceling headphones for Christmas. She's going to need them with both yowling
Holstein and yapping Poopsie in residence."

CHAPTER 32

THE NEXT MORNING PEGGY TIP-TOED DOWN-stairs so she wouldn't wake Stu. But when she looked in the living room the couch was empty, the sheets and blanket neatly folded on top of the pillow. Then she smelled fresh-brewed coffee. She walked into her kitchen and found Stu sitting at the table, staring into his coffee cup. Peggy bent down and gave Stu a quick hug before filling her own cup.

"You okay, Stu? You sleep well?"

Stu looked up at Peggy. "Thanks for putting me up last night. I don't know what I would have done without you."

"That's what friends are for. We help each other. Ian left some shaving stuff for you in the downstairs bathroom. Go upstairs and use the shower whenever you want."

"Thanks." Stu rubbed his hand over his stubbled

face. "I feel pretty scruffy. I think Emily would be a lot happier if I showered and shaved."

Peggy smiled. "I don't think a little beard burn is going to bother Emily. Ian will be here at eight, so you two can head over to the county jail together."

"I've been doing a lot of thinking this morning," said Stu as he refilled his coffee cup. "I feel like my life is just beginning. And I feel good about it. Is that so wrong?"

Peggy chose her words carefully. "I don't think it's wrong at all. You haven't had it easy, Stu. It's your turn for the brass ring. Grab it and be happy. We all deserve to be happy."

"Are you happy, Peggy Jean?"

"I'm working on it."

"You and Ian?"

Peggy shrugged. "Maybe. I'm not rushing into anything permanent."

"Maybe you should." Stu reached over to take Peggy's hand. "Why wasn't I smart enough to fall in love with you?"

Peggy smiled. "Because I'm the sister you never had. I will always love you, Stu, but I'm not in love with you. You know what I mean?"

"Yeah. I know what you mean. If it were going to happen for us, it would have happened a long time ago. Like it did for Chuck and Lavinia in high school, and for you and Tom."

Peggy's eyes welled at the memories. "Tom's been a tough act to follow."

"Don't wait too long, Peggy Jean. You can't live on memories. You need someone to love, and I want to take my sister down the aisle while I can still do it without a walker." Stu tapped Peggy affectionately on the tip of her nose, then pulled her into his arms in a warm, brotherly hug. "I love you, Peggy Jean."

"I love you, too, Stu."

Nicky coughed in the kitchen doorway.

"Hey, Nicky." Turning to Peggy, Stu said, "Okay if I use the shower now?"

"Sure. There are clean towels in the cupboard next to the bathroom. Help yourself."

Stu bounded upstairs, whistling under his breath.

Nicky sat at the kitchen table, a puzzled look on his face. "Mom, can I ask you something?"

"Sure, honey. What?"

"Are you and Mr. McIntyre going to get married?"

"No, honey. I think Stu is going to marry Emily."

"But I just saw you hugging. And heard all that mushy 'I love you' stuff."

Peggy sat next to Nicky and looked into her son's eyes. "Nicky, there are different kinds of love. I tell you 'I love you' all the time. That's the love of a mother for her son. When I said 'I love you' to Stu, that was the love of one good friend for another. That's all Stu and I are, honey. Good friends. We've known each other so long we're like brother and sister friends. Friends like you and Charlie."

"What about you and Ian?" asked Nicky.

"That's a different kind of love."

"Do you love him, Mom?"

"I think so, Nicky. How do you feel about that?"

Nicky thought for a minute. "That's cool, Mom. I like Ian. He doesn't play baseball or do stuff with me like Mr. McIntyre, but Ian knows about other things I like to do, like stamps and computers. He's smart and helps me with homework. That's neat, too."

"Okay!" Peggy held up her hand palm out. She and Nicky high-fived.

Nicky got up to grab a cereal bowl from the cupboard. "It would be neat to have a dad, Mom. Then when I marry Maria, you won't be all alone like old Mrs. McIntyre."

From the mouths of babes, thought Peggy. How does Nicky know that image scares me, too? "Nicky, you're eleven. You have lots of time before you get married. You'll meet many girls before then. Girls you don't even know now. What makes you so sure you're going to marry Maria?"

When Nicky looked at Peggy, she saw Tom in Nicky's face, hair, and eyes. And she heard in Nicky's voice the same intensity and passion that had been in Tom's voice that night in high school when he told Peggy he loved her and one day would marry her.

"Aw, Mom. Some things you just know."

Ten minutes later, Stu came back into the kitchen, showered, shaved, smelling good, and looking years younger than he had the day before.

"I was thinking, Peggy. I'm going to need a place to live." Stu smiled. "That is, I hope Emily and I will need a place to live."

"You have your mother's house," said Peggy.

"I'm putting it on the market," said Stu. "I want to start fresh and clean. In a house with no bad memories. I was looking across the street at the Murphy house. Is that still for rent?"

"Sure is, Stu. Lavinia and I are the rental agents for Gerald and Sara. We cleaned it last week and put on fresh linens when we took out all of Prunella Post's belongings." Peggy paused. "Knowing Prunella was there for a few days won't spoil it for Emily, will it?" Peggy smiled. "I can call in an exterminator—or an exorcist—if that'll help close the deal."

"Have you got time to show me the house?"

"Now?"

"Just a quick tour. I've never been inside."

Peggy looked at the clock. "Ian will be here in fifteen minutes. Give me two seconds to get dressed and we'll run over. Nicky, you okay on breakfast?"

Nicky gave his mother a thumbs-up.

By the time Ian arrived to go with Stu to spring Emily from the county jail, Peggy had a signed six-month lease for the Murphy house and a check from Stu for first, last, and the security deposit in her hand.

CHAPTER 33

STU AND EMILY WALKED ARM IN ARM INTO TOM'S Tools about lunchtime.

"We want to invite you to a wedding," said Emily. "But first I want to apologize to you, Peggy."

"You have nothing to apologize for, Emily. You were caught up in ugly circumstances. I'm very glad that everything worked out all right. Now, tell me about the wedding!"

"We just came from having a late breakfast with Max at the inn," said Stu. "We're being married Thursday morning. But not on the village green."

"Gee," said Peggy, smiling. "I can't imagine why you don't want to be married on the green. Aside from the weather factor."

Stu grinned, looking like his old self. "We're getting married in the Congregational church at eleven on Thanksgiving morning. Chuck is going to be my best man."

"I'd like you to be my matron of honor, Peggy. Would you?"

"It would be my pleasure," said Peggy. "What do you want me to wear? Two days isn't much time to make all the arrangements."

"Max is taking care of everything," said Stu. "He wants us to wear our colonial costumes."

Peggy began to laugh. "Oh, let me guess. Because the tourists will love it?"

"The important thing is that Emily and I are getting married," said Stu. "The rest is just window dressing. Max is paying for everything. Whatever he wants, he gets. Friday morning Emily and I are going to Paris on our honeymoon. That's another reason we wanted to talk to you."

"Two's company and three's a crowd, Stu. But thanks for thinking of me."

"We'll send you a postcard from Paris." Stu laughed and hugged Emily. "We wondered if you'll look after the Murphy house for us while we're away. We'll only be gone a few days. Emily starts her new teaching job the first week in December. She's going to teach sixth grade at Cobb's Landing elementary."

"You'll have Nicky and Charlie in your class, Emily. I'm warning you, they can be a handful. Don't worry about the house, Stu; I'll take care of it. You two go to Paris and have a wonderful time. When are you moving in?"

"This afternoon. Did you have a chance to make the extra keys?"

Peggy handed Stu and Emily two shiny new key rings with a bright brass key on each ring. "Here you are. Welcome to the neighborhood."

Stu reached for his wallet. "What do I owe you?"

Peggy waved away Stu's money offer. "Not a thing. Call it an engagement present."

Emily nudged Stu. "Ask Peggy about dinner."

"Emily wants to have a Thanksgiving dinner tonight. You and Ian, Lavinia and Chuck. And the boys, too, of course."

"The boys have pageant rehearsal tonight, and I can't speak for Ian, but I'd love to come."

"We already talked to Ian," said Emily. "He said yes, if you were free. Lavinia and Chuck said yes, too."

"Great. What time? What can I bring?"

"Just yourself. Six thirty all right?"

"Perfect."

Late Tuesday afternoon Peggy and Lavinia walked over to the village green to judge the snowman competition.

"Lovey, are you ready to eat more turkey tonight?"

"You know, PJ, I never thought I'd say this, but I think I'll be glad when this week is over. As much as I love Thanksgiving, there's only so much you can do with turkey leftovers, and I'm running out of ideas fast."

They walked around the green, looking at the remaining snow people. Finally they picked a winner. "Look it up on the list, PJ. Who built it?"

Peggy consulted her clipboard. "It was one of Freddy's. He didn't need to cheat, he would have won anyway."

"What do we do now, PJ?"

"We're going back to the store and draw a name out of hat. At this point I don't care who wins."

That night they all went to Stu and Emily's for Thanksgiving dinner, prepared to eat more turkey even if the very thought was making most of them gag. They were very pleasantly surprised when Emily served prime rib and Yorkshire pudding.

"It's what we always had for Thanksgiving when I was growing up," said Emily. "My mother hated turkey; she never knew what to do with all the left-overs."

CHAPTER 34

AT FIVE ON THE DOT WEDNESDAY AFTERNOON, the day before Thanksgiving, Peggy and Nicky were standing in the reception area at the inn. They were dressed in warm clothing—jeans, boots, sweaters, and down jackets and had mittens and hats tucked in their pockets.

The downstairs sitting area was full of tourists enjoying the view of the Rock River in the waning light of the setting sun. A cheerful fire blazed in the stone fireplace.

Peggy checked her watch for the tenth time.

"Where are we going, Mom?"

"Nicky, I haven't the faintest idea. All I know is that Max said you and I were to meet him here at five and dress warm because we going to be outside."

Peggy went to the reception desk. "Barbara, I'm looking for Max. Have you seen him?"

"No, Peggy, I haven't seen Max in several hours. He's very busy getting everything ready for tomorrow. Did you have an appointment?"

"I thought I did. I guess I was mistaken. Come on, Nicky, let's go home."

"Looking for someone?" There stood Ian, dressed in warm clothing similar to what Peggy and Nicky were wearing.

"I was supposed to meet Max, but he's not here," said Peggy.

"Actually, you were supposed to meet me, not Max. But that's part of the surprise. Are you ready to go?"

"Go where?"

Ian grinned. "That's for me to know, and you to find out." He steered them toward the entrance doors. "Our ride is waiting." He led Peggy and Nicky to the helicopter pad not far from the inn parking lot. There sat the helicopter Ian referred to as Air Max. The pilot stood next to the door.

Nicky's eyes grew as big as saucers. He turned to Ian. "Are we going for a ride in that?"

Ian smiled and put his arm around Nicky's shoulders. "Yes, Nicky, we are. And that's only part of the surprise." Ian turned to the pilot. "We're ready when you are. You know our destination."

"I've already filed the flight plan, sir. We've got clear weather all the way."

Nicky sat up front next to the pilot, while Ian and Peggy sat together in the back.

Within seconds they were rising in the air over Cobb's Landing.

"Wow!" said Nicky. "Hey, look, Mom! You can see our house. I can even see Buster running around in the back yard."

Peggy had never seen Cobb's Landing from the air. She looked out the window, her nose pressed against the glass, until the little toy town disappeared from view. Ahead, the southeast sky dimmed to inky black, and below them were the twinkling lights of houses, cars, and street lamps. Like Nicky, Peggy was too awed to speak.

As the trip progressed, the ground lights grew brighter and more numerous. In the far distance the horizon was aglow with lights that stretched high in the sky.

"Have you guessed where we're headed?" asked Ian.

Peggy shook her head.

"All right, I'll give you a hint. What's one of your favorite parts of Thanksgiving?"

Peggy look at Ian and shrugged. Then she opened her mouth in surprise and delight and her face lit up. "The Macy's parade?"

Ian grinned. "Since you can't watch the parade live tomorrow, tonight I'm taking you and Nicky to the parade. You'll see the balloons being inflated, the floats being assembled, and you might even get to hear some of the bands practicing."

Peggy threw her arms around Ian and kissed him.

"I know how much you gave up to go along with Max's plans for Thanksgiving. And I also know how much you love the Macy's parade. Tonight was my idea, but Max made all the arrangements. This is his treat. His way of saying thank you." Ian opened a picnic hamper. "We'll have a snack now, then after we've seen everything we'll stop at the Carnegie Deli for corned beef sandwiches before we head home."

When the helicopter arrived in New York City, a limousine was waiting.

"Seventy-seventh and Central Park West," said Ian.

"Yes, sir," said the driver. "You must be pretty important. That whole area's blocked off because they're getting ready for the parade tomorrow. But the boss told me you've got special clearance."

The rest of the evening was a fantasy for both Peggy and Nicky. They nibbled on large hot pretzels from a street vendor and walked for blocks looking at everything. They saw the Garfield and Mr. Monopoly balloons being inflated, covered by giant nets anchored by sandbags; they watched the Tom Turkey float that led the parade being assembled, and Nicky even got to sit in Santa's seat on the giant snow goose sleigh that ended the parade.

"Oh, I wish Maria were here," said Nicky.

Ian put away his camera and pulled a cell phone from his jacket pocket. "Call her, Nicky. Tell her where you are. I'll dial the number for you." Ian punched in the numbers and handed the phone to Nicky.

While Nicky talked to Maria, Ian and Peggy stood with their arms around each other's waists. Ian looked at his watch. "We've got one more stop to make before we get something to eat."

Back in the limo, Ian said two words to the driver: "Herald Square."

They drove down Central Park West to Columbus Circle, then down Broadway, past Times Square— Peggy giggled when she saw the 42nd Street sign- post. "It's just like the Busby Berkeley movie! My mother loved that movie so much; that's why she named me Peggy. After Peggy Sawyer. 'You're going out there a youngster, but you're going to come back a star.' I can still hear my mother saying that to me when I was growing up." They finally ar- rived at Herald Square.

Ian showed his identification to the guards. Then he, Peggy, and Nicky were taken to a roped-off area where they watched the bands rehearse, saw some of the Broadway show numbers that would appear dur- ing the parade, and for a final treat watched the Rockettes rehearse their routine.

In the limo on the way to the Carnegie Deli, Peggy turned to Ian. "I wish I knew how to say more than thank you. Tonight has been a night Nicky and I will never forget."

Ian kissed Peggy softly, then whispered in her ear, "This is just the beginning, Peggy Jean. We'll con- tinue this conversation tomorrow."

CHAPTER 35

THANKSGIVING MORNING DAWNED CRISP AND clear. When Peggy got down to the kitchen to make coffee, Nicky was already there eating his breakfast.

"Happy Thanksgiving, Nicky."

"Happy Thanksgiving, Mom." Nicky looked at Peggy with stars in his eyes. "Wasn't last night neat?"

Peggy stopped filling the coffee pot to look at her son. "Yes, Nicky. It was neat. It was wonderful. A once-in-a-lifetime treat."

"Oh, I know that, Mom. It was like Disneyworld. But you can't live in Disneyworld. I'm glad we live right here in Cobb's Landing. New York City is really dirty. But I liked the hot pretzels and the sandwiches and the big pickles."

Peggy resumed filling the coffee pot, thankful on the day of giving thanks that Nicky had a good head on his shoulders and a solid sense of values.

"I have to be at the inn at eight, Mom. My part of the pageant isn't until later, but Max wants everyone there on time. You'll be there to see me?"

"I promised I would, Nicky. Then we're all going to Stu and Emily's wedding at eleven."

"And dinner starts at one. More turkey. I can't wait. I love turkey."

"I'm glad, honey. We have a lot of leftovers to finish."

When Nicky had left for the inn with Charlie and Chuck, Peggy dressed for the day in her colonial costume. As she stood looking in the mirror, she thought about the first Thanksgiving. Not the Cobb's Landing first Thanksgiving in 1863, but the 1621 Thanksgiving—or the legend of that purported event. Would I have been brave enough to survive the hardships that the pilgrims endured? Would I have wanted to spend my days chopping wood, hauling water, cooking over a fire? Worrying about lack of food, illness, and wild animals? No, Peggy decided, she would not. She was thankful to be living in Cobb's Landing in the present, and if the tourists wanted to believe in the myth of Colonial Village, then Peggy was going to do everything she could to ensure they had a good time, because her livelihood depended on it. She smoothed the starched white apron over the butternut-brown long skirt, applied some blush and lip gloss, brushed her hair, and reached for her woolen shawl.

Max's horse-drawn sleighs were already clip-clopping up and down Main Street as Peggy joined the other costumed residents heading on foot for the inn. We really do look like pilgrims, Peggy thought.

The ground floor of the inn had been transformed overnight into a mini-theater, complete with a small raised stage and rows of folding chairs for the audience. Most of the seats had been taken by tourists, so Peggy and Lavinia stood with the other pilgrims on the sidelines.

Max bounded to center stage and made a short welcoming speech, then he moved to a podium off to the side where he became the narrator for the series of sketches that made up his Thanksgiving pageant. Overall, the pageant was corny but cute; the schoolchildren were adorable in their costumes and the tourists ate it up. They applauded everything and adored Maria as Priscilla Alden.

That could be my future daughter-in-law, thought Peggy, hoping that whomever Nicky married would be as sweet as Maria.

When the pageant was over, coffee and pumpkin muffins were set out on long tables and the folding chairs quickly removed.

It was now time for Stu and Emily's wedding. Peggy and Ian joined Lavinia and Chuck for a ride in one of the sleighs up to the Congregational church near the old cemetery. Ian was dressed in his Colonial Village costume, and Peggy remembered the first time she'd seen Ian in that costume and how her cheeks had flushed when Lavinia teased her about how sexy Ian looked. Peggy looked over at Lavinia and winked. Lavinia grinned.

When they reached the church, Stu and Emily were standing outside chatting with Max. Emily looked radiant and lovely in her colonial costume.

Instead of a veil, or that dorky hat, her head was adorned with a simple wreath of flowers.

As they got out of the sleigh, Peggy turned to look down Main Street toward the Rock River. Approaching the church were a steady stream of people, some in sleighs, some walking in small groups. Pilgrims, Indians, tourists. Soon the small church was packed to overflowing. Latecomers stood outside the open doors to listen to the ceremony. Ian and Lavinia sat together in the front pew while Peggy and Chuck performed their duties as attendants to the bride and groom. Max, dressed in a well-tailored gray suit and his usual red silk bow tie, gravely escorted Emily down the aisle, kissed her gently on the cheek, then placed her hand in Stu's.

There was only one hymn sung that morning. "We Gather Together" resounded throughout the small church. Some of the singers were off-key, some forgot the words, but the sentiment of fellowship and thanksgiving was heartfelt.

When the simple marriage service was over, Stu and Emily walked sedately down the aisle and into the sunshine where they were showered with bird-seed thrown by the wedding guests. Max had thought of everything.

Ian pulled Peggy back into the church. He led her to a deserted pew and waited for a minute until the church was almost empty. Then he took Peggy's hand in his. "This is where we left off last night. I think the next wedding in Cobb's Landing should be ours. I love you, Peggy, and I promise to be a good father to Nicky. Will you marry me?"

Peggy looked deep into Ian's sky-blue eyes. What she saw was love, sincerity, passion, and a good heart. Here was a man she could grow old with and love to her dying day. "Yes, I will marry you."

Ian pulled an engagement ring from his vest pocket and placed it on Peggy's finger. Then he kissed her.

They heard muted applause and turned to see Lavinia, Chuck, and Max standing in the doorway to the church, smiling their approval.

"Don't forget, PJ," said Lavinia. "I get to be the flower girl."

CHAPTER 36

AT THE END OF THE DAY, AS THE SUN WAS ONCE again casting its waning light onto the Rock River, when the turkeys were nothing but bones and slivers of meat, the pumpkin pies reduced to crumbs, and the tourists were queuing at the reception desk to make early reservations for the following year's colonial Thanksgiving feast, Peggy finally had a private moment outside with Max.

"Well, Mayor, it all turned out pretty well, don't you think? Now we've got people clamoring to be married here. A whole new sideline for Colonial Village."

"Yes, Max, everything worked. It was a perfect Thanksgiving. But there's still one mystery left unsolved."

"Oh? And what is that?"

"I never did find out who broke my store window."

Max looked vaguely uncomfortable and cleared his throat.

"Furball problem, Max?"

Max mumbled something Peggy couldn't hear over the splash of water on the slowly turning water wheel.

"Speak up, Max. I didn't hear what you said."

"I broke your window."

Peggy stared at Max. "You did it? Why?"

"Because you wouldn't go along with my Thanksgiving plans and I wanted to teach you a lesson." Max handed Peggy a folded check. "This will pay for your new window."

Peggy put the check in her pocket and then looked at Max for a long moment. "Max, you really are a devil."

Max smiled. A smile as inscrutable as the *Mona Lisa*, as old as the sphinx. He straightened his red silk bow tie before replying softly, "I never said I wasn't."

The setting sun behind Max created a reddish aura that enveloped him completely. In that brief instant, Peggy could have sworn she saw two little red horns on Max's head and heard the swish of his red forked tail. She blinked and the illusion disappeared.

With a wink and a wave, Max was gone.

KATE BORDEN

Welcome to COBB'S LANDING

DEATH OF A TART
The first book in the
Peggy Turner mystery series!

As mayor of Cobb's Landing, Peggy Jean Turner is
thrilled with the idea of creating "Colonial
Williamsburg" in the bankrupt town.
All goes swimmingly, until the town tart
turns up dead—and Peggy must risk everything
to solve the crime.

0-425-19489-2

And don't miss
DEATH OF A TRICKSTER
0-425-19946-0

PC992

Big Crimes on Campus

by Ann Waldron
•Include recipes for faculty events!•

The Princeton Murders
0-425-18820-5

For Professor McLeod Delaney, the hallowed halls of
Princeton University offer an unexpected education in
murder when English professors are targeted by an
intellectual with a grudge.

Death of a Princeton President
0-425-19462-0

When Princeton University's first female president is
strangled, Professor McLeod Delaney must face the
administration's stonewalling and a host of shady suspects
to discover who placed her highly-esteemed former
colleague on permanent sabbatical.

**Available wherever books are sold or at
penguin.com**